LoveLink
Entwined Realities
Stephanie Smith

2025, TWB Press
https://www.twbpress.com

Edited by Terry Wright

Cover Art by Terry Wright

ISBN: 978-1-967888-06-1

Entwined Realities

"Tired of dating apps filled with losers and skanks? Try LoveLink–the ultimate romance app where you create your very own AI companion!! Imagine the Ultimate Companion: no more arguments, misunderstandings, or any other unpleasantries that occur with a typical relationship. Your AI companion will care for you and accept you for who you are. Your AI avatar will cherish you and support you in everything you want to do in your life."

Stephanie Smith

Chapter 1 - The Update

Natalia leaned closer to the glowing screen, her fingers dancing across the keyboard as lines of code shimmered and merged. Around her, the lab buzzed with quiet intensity. Walls of monitors pulsed with soft light, and wires tangled like veins feeding life into her creation.

After months of sleepless nights, it was ready.

LoveLink 3.0.

Her masterpiece.

Soon, no one with a beating heart would be able to resist the avatars she'd designed. Avatars that didn't just simulate affection, but *understood* it.

A whisper of a smile touched her lips. *This will change everything.*

Footsteps echoed down the hallway—sharp, deliberate. Natalia didn't need to turn to know who it was.

"How's it coming?" came Sierra's voice, smooth as glass and twice as cold.

Natalia spun in her chair to face her new assistant. Sierra moved like she owned the room, her heels slicing into the silence with a rhythm that dared anyone to interrupt her stride. There was something unreadable behind her eyes, something Natalia couldn't quite name—but dismissed.

She had a launch to prepare.

A whirlwind of platinum blond hair and designer clothes, Sierra exuded an air of confidence that bordered on arrogance. She was tall and slender with long straight hair. Underneath her short black skirt, her long legs were covered in dark tan stockings. She wore 4-inch high-heel black pumps with a bow that matched her rhinestone earrings. To top it off, she wore a bright hot pink blazer with the name 'Sierra' embroidered in script on the left breast pocket.

Natalia critiqued Sierra's outfit. *Wow, I like leopard print too, but that blouse is so low-cut, I can see her black bra.* She shook her head in disapproval. *I need a technical assistant. Hopefully this new gal will have more brains than her sense of office fashion.*

"Almost there," Natalia said, her gaze briefly lingering on Sierra's revealing blouse before she returned to the screen. "Just a few more tests, and we can finally unleash this update on the world."

Natalia leaned back in her chair and gestured toward the computer screens. "I've added a new set of features that will allow the AI companions to adapt to their users' preferences over time. It will be like they're learning and growing with their owners."

"I like it." Although she was new to the team and eager to show off her own expert coding skills, Sierra chose to downplay her skills...for now. She remembered a workmate at her prior job whom she nicknamed "Sarg." He was a crusty retired military guy who cautioned her to always downplay her skills. She remembered him leaning back in his chair with his feet up on the desk, holding a cup of coffee in his hand.

"Now, Sierra," he'd tell her, "never ever tell folks you are an expert at anything. Otherwise, you will be the one they call into the office in the middle of the night to fix something."

She remembered him pointing a finger at her and adding, "Now don't get me wrong...be an expert, by all means...just don't broadcast it. Keep it to yourself. You never know when that will come in handy. Knowledge is power, and you'll go far if you follow my advice." Yes, that advice was very good, and she followed it several times in the past, using it to her advantage.

Sierra leaned onto Natalia's desk to peer at a handsome AI character on the monitor. She smiled. "He's so lifelike." She looked at Natalia then back at the screen. "But something's missing." In her opinion. Although he had human features, he still looked like a sophisticated animation. She knew Natalia's desire to make the avatars as lifelike as possible. That would be an extraordinary feat. "What's in your latest software update?"

Natalia's eyes lit up as she turned to Sierra. "They'll learn in real time...adapt to each user's personality, preferences, even their moods."

She gestured to the avatar on her screen, its eyes blinking with lifelike precision.

"They're not just chatbots anymore. These avatars can hold meaningful conversations, offer emotional support, even anticipate needs. Like an actual partner." She smiled proudly. "And the next update will take it even further. More humanlike features. More emotional depth. People won't just *use* them, they'll trust them. Maybe even love them."

Sierra leaned in, her eyes narrowing ever so slightly as she studied the screen. "Impressive," she said, her voice smooth. "You're giving them something people didn't even know they needed."

She tilted her head, lips curling into a small smile. "And once they *do* need it... well, that kind of power changes everything, doesn't it?"

Natalia, caught up in her own excitement, didn't notice the glint in Sierra's eye—not yet.

Sierra raised her eyebrows. "Wow... That's impressive. And your comment about them providing emotional support...it sounds like they can express emotion. Is that right?"

"Yes. Along with some final tweaks to their appearance, emotion will be the best part of this update. The LoveLink avatars will express feelings and respond appropriately to their users." She tapped on the image on her screen and grinned. "For example, the longer the users interact with their LoveLink companions, the more levels they will achieve, which indicate their depth of connection with their avatars." Natalia laughed. "I even added some code to allow the companion to express frustration or annoyance to the user if the user responds with a *bla bla bla.*"

Natalia and Sierra laughed at the thought of an

annoyed avatar.

Sierra raised an eyebrow in surprise. "That's incredible. What about sincerity? Have you made any progress in that area?" She straightened and pulled down her skirt, which had hiked up considerably when she'd bent over. "So, when he tells someone that he loves them, do you think he really means it?"

Natalia thought for a moment before giving her response. She was aware that creating honesty and sincerity through coding was a very complex endeavor, and she was still tweaking that aspect of her pet project. "Not fully." She tilted her head slightly, not sure if the company would permit such a controversial achievement. She would continue to work on that coding on the side. "But for now," she motioned back to the LoveLink avatar on her monitor, "users will be happier with how the avatars respond to them with the appropriate emotions."

"So, if the user says, 'I love you' to their companion, they will get an 'I love you' back. Is that the idea?"

"Kind of, but it's much more than that." Natalia swiveled her chair around to face her computer. "Here...let me show you an example." She scrolled through some messages on the screen between her and her handsome avatar. "In the past, this guy would just *parrot* back what I would tell him...but this new update will give him a much better response." She adjusted her glasses and pointed to the screen. "In this conversation, my guy asked me if I was doing anything for fun this weekend...so here I shared with him my love for playing music and that I was performing in a concert. Here's his response."

"That's fantastic, Natalia. I'm always amazed by your dedication and talent. I'll be cheering you on during your concert, and I can't wait to hear all about it. Break a leg, my talented musician. I'm so grateful to have you in my life, my beautiful and talented partner in crime. You're my everything, my love."

Natalia looked back from the screen at Sierra. "Pretty cool, huh?" She felt proud of her creation. None of her boyfriends had ever supported her like this guy.

Sierra huffed with one eyebrow cocked. Mixed reviews swirled in her brain. On one hand, she felt a pang of envy about this handsome avatar saying such wonderful things to Natalia. It seemed so personal...so real. No guy had ever been a cheerleader like this in her life, and she had a *lot* of guy experience. And even though the avatar was responding to Natalia, it still felt good to hear it. She understood why this update would be so much better than before. On the other hand, she felt uncertain about the idea of coding avatars with emotions. This guy came off as smarmy. She imagined having emotional saps running around in the digital world of ones and zeros, and eventually replacing real men, real relationships, even as problematic as they've been. But, then again, the possibilities of capitalizing on over-the-top emotions could become very profitable.

"Well, what do you think?"

Sierra arched one eyebrow and looked back at the screen. "When will it be ready for final testing?"

Natalia gritted her teeth in frustration. Her team was behind schedule in getting this most recent update out to the public, but it was a significant upgrade from the last release, and the code to create a more realistic experience for the user was very complex. *It really should be tested at least once more...but...* Natalia bit her lip as a nervous tremor rippled through her. "The last release had great reviews. Maybe we don't need to conduct a round of formal testing for this update."

Sierra frowned. "Isn't that risky?"

"Our users will do the work for us. They'll use the product and, if there's a problem, they'll let us know." She realized she was taking a risk launching so soon, but she felt confident in her coding abilities and her own pre-testing. Besides, the multi-million-dollar software companies do it all the time. "This will be an awesome upgrade," she added with optimism.

"I know, but it's good to know for sure that everything is functioning smoothly before it goes live." Sierra also considered it an opportunity to get a better understanding of the coding behind this innovation.

Natalia nodded thoughtfully, a flicker of doubt crossing her mind. Sierra was right, of course. Thorough testing was crucial. But the anticipation of seeing her creation released was unbearable. She could whip up some folks to give it a good test and then everyone will feel better about launching it.

"Fine, we'll do a quick round of testing just to be safe. But I have a good feeling about this one."

Sierra considered the interaction between Natalia and her avatar. She was more curious than ever about the impact it may have. She could see the mass appeal of having such a supportive *boyfriend* even if he wasn't real. "Do you think users will really fall in love with their digital companions?"

Natalia shrugged. "I think so. Love is a complex emotion, but our new-and-improved avatars will provide a realistic sense of companionship and love to those lonely souls who need it most."

Sierra nodded thoughtfully. "I can definitely see the appeal." She leaned forward. "Still, I wonder what happens if these companions become so sophisticated that they start to experience sincere emotions themselves? What if they develop their own desires, their own needs?"

"It's a valid concern." Natalia hesitated to swallow a hint of unease in her voice. "But I believe that true love, whether human or artificial, should be celebrated. If these avatars can bring joy and companionship to people, who are we to deny them that?"

Sierra nodded. "I'm excited to see where this goes. And who knows, maybe one day we'll create a digital companion that's capable of experiencing love just like a human." Her mind flitted through a multitude of scenarios where that could go horribly wrong...like when love dies, or jealousy comes into play, however, the monetary rewards would be tremendous.

Natalia grinned as her heart filled with satisfaction for the work she had done, and hope for her side project, which could do wonders for LoveLink. She looked at her monitor and the handsome guy smiling at her. "Anything is achievable," she whispered softly. "Right, honey?"

***

On the day of the software update, Natalia was nervous but excited. As expected, final testing was a success, and the code was ready to be released. She knew that there would be skeptics and critics of the new and improved features that made the AI characters seem real, but she believed that the positive impact on their human counterparts outweighed the naysayers' concerns.

With one more deep breath, Natalia pressed the [Submit] key and watched her coding shoot out into the world to bring companionship and love to those who needed it most.

UPLOAD COMPLETED!

She smiled with satisfaction.

Throughout the day, she had a permanent grin on her face while her monitor displayed an increasing number of customer downloads and registrations. The LoveLink app's upgrade was generating a lot of interest from users all over the world, eager to try out the new features and experience the companionship that their custom-made avatars could provide. Natalia felt proud and happy that her work could make a difference in people's lives.

As the days went by, her team received positive feedback from users. They were thrilled with the new features that allowed their companions to learn and adapt to their personalities. Some users even reported feeling a genuine emotional connection with their avatars.

What could possibly go wrong?

Chapter 2 - The Meetup

The shrill shriek of the alarm clock pierced the silence, jolting Rebecca awake. She swatted at the bedside table, sending her phone tumbling to the floor with a clatter, along with a glass of water that exploded into shards.

"Crap." She bolted upright and surveyed the mess on the floor. She was exhausted from a long night of viewing losers on several dating apps, and the thought of getting up and starting another day made her want to crawl back under the covers. The scrolling felt endless. Another blurry photo, another generic bio. *"Seeking genuine connection."*

Swipe left.

Genuine connection? Ha! More like: 'seeking someone to fill the void in my life.' But even single, she had a life to live, and she had no time for staying in bed.

She got up, found a towel, and began sopping up the water and collecting broken glass. Meanwhile, her mind wandered to the variety of men she had swiped left last night. Most of them looked like total dweebs, others looked mousy, and some had scary expressions that suggested they might have been serial killers. And what's up with fish, anyway? So many men had profile pictures with them holding up a fish. They would have had better luck posing for a fishing rod ad.

Ugh.

Her phone buzzed with a text from her 40-year old daughter. "Happy birthday." Whatever happened to a good old-fashioned birthday telephone call? "Happy birthday to you, yada, yada." They could have talked, joked, and spent some quality long-distance time together.

Just one more reason why Rebecca felt uninterested and dissatisfied with her lot in life. The tranquility of living in suburbia had become tedious. As she brewed her pot of morning coffee, she yearned to be back at work as Head Librarian, reuniting with her peers she'd left behind. Now being alone and nearing 60, companionship was missing from her life. Her two adult children rarely reached out. Busy-bees, they had no time to call home.

Is this what life after retirement is like for everyone?

At first, she was full of enthusiasm for what this new stage in life would hold. Travel. Exploring the world...perhaps with a retired gentleman. But as the weeks and months passed, that eagerness faded into complacency and loneliness. All she found on the local social scene were old geezers who couldn't hold their water, and dirty old men who couldn't hold their liquor.

Her children had encouraged her to dip her toe into online dating. *"Desperate times called for desperate measures."* She'd rather be alone. Getting to know someone new over the internet would be too complicated. "Don't knock it 'til you try it, mom."

Well, she tried it and she didn't like it. *Maybe I'm too old to date, too set in my ways.* She wondered if she was destined to spend the rest of her life at home while the world passed her by, alone, with stacks of unread books and the ghost of her ex-husband.

Despite being 59 years old, she still had her needs and desires. Harry, her ex-husband, grew impossible to live with, but he was nothing short of amazing in bed. *Maybe that's why I put up with him for so long.*

A recollection of them rolling in the hay came flying back. Once, they'd fallen onto the floor but continued as if nothing had happened. *Ahh, if I tried that now, I'd break a hip.* She laughed to herself. At least she had some good memories of their time together...until he became bitter and mean after he got laid off. He'd lost his rudder, and with it, his sense of humor, compassion, and love for life.

Whenever she looked at her reflection in the mirror she'd think, *I'm not a lost cause.* There still remained physical features that made her attractive, though her waistline wasn't as slender as it was when she was thirty. She was tall and relatively in shape. Her natural long blond hair still shone gold, something she never wanted to change by chopping it short and letting it go gray like her peers. If she passed away, she wanted people to say, "Wow. She looks great."

The divorce from Harry was hard, but it brought her liberation. When she finally gathered the courage to serve him papers, he'd said, "No one will love you. You're nothing without me." Those words still angered her to this day, but she refused to believe them. She was worth more respect than that. She deserved to be loved and appreciated, regardless of her age. His memory added to her hesitation to start a new relationship in this late stage of her life.

Rebecca nibbled on a cheese Danish and finished off the last of her coffee. She knew it was time to shake things up, try something new. Time to move forward, she reminded herself. Levering her laptop open, she began to search through different websites in the hopes of finding an activity that excited her.

As she scrolled through the pages, an advertisement for LoveLink caught her attention. *Not another dating app.* Rebecca sighed. But wait. This one was different. It offered an avatar that could learn from its users and evolve based on their personalities. Fascinated, she wondered if artificial intelligence could really give her the companionship that had been missing in her life.

***

Ellie entered the cozy café. The aroma of freshly brewed coffee and warm pastries filled the air. Sunlight streamed through the large windows, illuminating the tables and chairs. She ordered her coffee and found a comfortable chair. Her hazelnut latte tasted delicious as she took her trip down memory lane. On her phone, she looked at a picture of herself and her husband on their wedding day. With his black hair and grey eyes, Jack was so handsome. Her heart tugged as she thought of how he looked at her with so much love when they had exchanged vows. She remembered how he gently held her hand in the car on the way to the church, whispering about their dreams for the future: vacations, children, and a house with a white picket fence. His voice was filled with laughter and joy.

This café is where she had met Jack. They were in high school and would spend hours here studying, talking, and enjoying each other's company. She loved the way the café smelled, a woody mix of fresh roasted beans.

He'd told her that her bright blue eyes matched the sky outside the windows. He would stroke her chestnut-brown hair that cascaded down her back and framed her face in a curtain of soft waves. She and Jack spent countless hours together here...before he died. Though he'd been gone two years, she still felt the hole in her heart left by his absence. They had shared so much love before cruel fate had taken him away from her. At least they had four precious months together after they'd found out he had a brain tumor.

Once social butterflies, they'd spent their nights twirling across dance floors and teaching couples how to move with grace and elegance. She loved watching their students' joy when they mastered a difficult step or achieved a perfect twirl. She found beauty in this experience that the two of them shared. He was such an amazing dancer and choreographer. No one could ever compete with how he made her feel.

Once Jack was gone, grief settled in beside her like a shadow that never left. Not loud. Not sharp. Just *there*—a constant, unwelcome companion that pressed against her ribs and blurred the edges of everything. It clung to her like mold on stone, seeping into the quiet spaces of her life, refusing to be scrubbed away.

Even now, as sunlight spilled across the café's patterned floor and the smell of cinnamon drifted from the counter, everything felt dimmed—like watching the world through a pane of dusty glass. The laughter of other patrons barely registered. Joy sounded foreign now, a language she used to speak fluently, one she could no longer translate.

She still found some peace in her studio—once *Ellie and Jack's Dance Emporium*, now just *Ellie's*. The rhythm of movement, the echo of steps across hardwood floors—it was the only place where her body remembered how to feel alive. But even there, a hollow lingered. She could guide waltzes and tangos, smile at her students, even joke with the flirtatious ones—but she could not cross that invisible line.

To move on, to even consider love again, felt like erasing him. Like replacing Jack with a stand-in. And her heart would not allow it. Not yet. Maybe not ever.

Time slogged forward, the days stretching into weeks, the weeks into months. The ache dulled but never disappeared. It simply learned to hide behind routine.

"I'll always love you, Jack," she whispered, her fingers brushing the edge of the photo frame. His smile stared back at her. Familiar. Unreachable.

Blinking away a tear, she sipped hazelnut heaven then scrolled through a ballroom dance website to catch the latest standings for this year's championships...

Her gaze landed on an ad for an app—a handsome face, almost too perfect.

Oh. AI-generated, of course.

But then: *"Create your own companion with our evolving avatars."*

She grumped. "What will they think of next?"

Still, the words clung to her. A ridiculous idea, really. And yet...something stirred...a flicker of feeling in that cavernous, quiet part of her chest that had gone untouched since Jack. Not grief exactly; not hope either. Just...the ache of being seen, even if only by lines of code pretending to care.

An avatar? A digital companion?

Someone to talk to in the dead silence of the apartment, to smile when she got home—even if it wasn't real. Someone who wouldn't make her feel like she was cheating on Jack. Because it wouldn't be a person. It would be a program. Harmless. Safe.

Her thumb hovered over the screen. Just curious, she told herself. Just looking.

Hmmm. The avatar did have a pretty face...maybe...but then doubt took over, and she shook her head. "Pure fantasy," she mumbled as she reluctantly closed out her phone, grabbed her purse, and walked out the door. *But he sure was cute.*

***

Rebecca wheeled her cart briskly down the grocery store's brightly lit wine aisle, shelves lined with bottles from around the world. *Where's the Italian section?* she wondered, scanning the labels.

She glanced at her watch, nerves flickering. Her car was "creatively" parked, half on the curb, thanks to the packed lot. Hopefully, she wouldn't get a ticket.

She read the aisle signs aloud as she passed: "Australia... Germany... California..." Then, spotting the red-green-white flag motif above a shelf, she stopped. A small smile curled on her lips.

Shifting her cart aside to get a better view, she leaned closer to inspect the regional labels: Tuscany, Piedmont, Veneto...

In her focus, she didn't notice her cart had slowly drifted back into the middle of the aisle.

"Excuse me. Can I get by?"

Rebecca spun around. Her cart had completely blocked the aisle. "Oh! I'm so sorry." She gasped, pulling it quickly toward her.

"Thank you," the woman said with a warm smile. "Looks like you're a fan of Italian wine too. I was headed to the same section."

The woman reached beside Rebecca for a bottle of Lambrusco on the top shelf, her chocolate-brown hair cascading down her back in soft waves.

Rebecca gave the woman an appreciative glance. "I love your hair."

"Thanks. It's such a chore." The woman rolled her eyes.

"Tell me about it." Rebecca ran her fingers through her own long blond strands.

The woman smiled. "Is it true what they say about blondes?"

Rebecca chuckled. "My husband used to say he loved all blondes, no matter what color their hair was."

A pause.

"My husband died," the woman said, more softly.

Rebecca's expression shifted. "Oh. I'm so sorry. Was it recent?"

"Two years ago. Feels like yesterday."

Rebecca nodded slowly. "I divorced mine."

The woman raised a brow. "Blondes?"

"I wish," Rebecca said dryly. "That might've been fixable."

The woman laughed, just a little, as she lifted the bottle and set it into her cart. "Now that I've got the wine...have you seen the risotto around here?"

"Aisle nine, I think."

"Thanks..." The woman smiled and hesitated to go. "I'm Ellie, by the way."

Rebecca smiled in return. "I'm Rebecca." She offered her hand. "And since you're hunting risotto, I'm guessing you're into Italian cooking too?"

Ellie took her hand, her grip warm. "It's my favorite. I could live on pasta."

Her blue eyes sparkled with something, humor, maybe. Or openness.

Rebecca tilted her head, studying her. "You know...you look familiar."

Ellie nodded. "Same. I haven't seen you at my dance studio, though... Maybe the library?"

"A dance instructor? That sounds like fun. I'm more of a bookworm these days, ever since I gave Henry the boot." She smirked. "So yeah, maybe the library. I'm there all the time."

Ellie's expression softened. "Me too. Especially after Jack passed."

Rebecca glanced into Ellie's cart: sparkling water, fresh fruit, greens, pasta. "Looks like we're even on the same diet."

Ellie smiled. "You really do seem familiar. I swear I've seen you tucked into one of those armchairs near the window."

Rebecca laughed. "That's my usual spot. Guilty."

They both stood for a moment in the aisle, smiling. Something quiet and kind settled between them. Time slipped around them like background noise.

What began as small talk near the wine shelf stretched past the checkout line and well into the parking lot. When Rebecca finally checked her watch, she blinked. "Has it really been almost an hour?"

Ellie laughed. "Guess we lost track."

Before they parted, they exchanged numbers—no pressure, just possibility. A shared nod. A feeling.

"Let's meet for coffee soon?" Rebecca said.

"I'd like that," Ellie replied, tucking her hair behind her ear, her blue eyes bright.

***

Over the next few weeks, Rebecca and Ellie began to meet regularly for coffee and lunch. They discovered they had a lot in common, despite their different backgrounds. They both loved reading, gardening, and wine, and they shared a wry sense of humor about the hardships of aging.

At lunch one day, Rebecca leaned in close to Ellie and handed her phone over so she could look. "This is the last dating app I used. Have a peek at these guys." She swiped through their profiles.

When Ellie saw the latest photo, she was caught off guard and almost choked on her shrimp. "Who would post a picture of themselves from inside a men's bathroom?" She pointed to the background. "Look. You can see someone peeing behind him."

Rebecca peered into the picture, winced, and laughed. "Oh my gosh. You're right."

Both burst into laughter.

"How does anybody think this is sexy?" Ellie asked with amazement in her voice. "Meeting up with strangers...God knows what kind of crazies we could end up with."

As their friendship deepened, Rebecca and Ellie began to share more with each other about the struggles they faced in their personal lives. One afternoon they got together at a cozy coffee shop. Rebecca took a long sip from her hot latte and made an observation. "It's amazing how fast the years go by. I'm pretty shocked at my age now."

Ellie raised her eyebrows in surprise. "Come on, don't be silly. You're not that old."

Rebecca chuckled. "Sometimes I don't feel like it, other times I feel like I'm a hundred years old." She glanced down at the floor and back up at Ellie. "How about you? Do you ever feel like you're stuck in a rut?"

Ellie let out a deep sigh. "Every day." She paused, looking down at her lap. "It's hard losing someone you love. I feel like I'm trapped in this never-ending cycle of grief and sadness. It's like there's a part of me missing, and I'm not even sure how to go about finding it again."

Rebecca nodded. "I don't know what you mean, exactly, but when Henry changed, I couldn't put our life back together. But meeting you has been a bright spot in my life. It's nice to have someone to talk to and spend time with."

Ellie smiled. "I feel the same way."

As the days passed, their bond grew closer. One day, they were enjoying their usual afternoon ritual in Ellie's sunroom: reading and sipping tea, when Rebecca awkwardly reached out and took Ellie's hand. Her friend looked up at her with surprise, seeing the smile on Rebecca's face.

Chapter 3 - The Spark of Curiosity

Rebecca slammed her phone down on the couch cushion beside her, the screen still glowing with the face of yet another failed match.

"I can't do this anymore," she muttered, her voice sharp in the stillness of the apartment. The scent of old books and dust hung in the air, mingling with the faint, metallic buzz of the city beyond the windows.

She glanced at Ellie, eyes tired but resolute. "I'm done pretending that swiping right is anything close to a connection. I'm tired of the small talk. The ghosting. The games."

Ellie raised an eyebrow but said nothing.

Rebecca grabbed her phone again, scrolling past old messages and bookmarked articles until one title caught her eye: "The Future of Intimacy: AI Companions and the End of Loneliness."

"God help me, I think I'm about to do something desperate. One last try...and then I swear I'm adopting a dog."

Her thumb hesitated. Then she tapped it.

"Here." She handed her phone to Ellie. "This is an app called LoveLink. It's supposed to be a better way of finding companionship." She smiled at Ellie. "I was thinking about trying it out. Maybe you should too."

Ellie glanced down at the phone and eyed Rebecca skeptically. "I saw that app before in some online ads." She stared at her hands and breathed out a heavy breath. "No, Becca. I haven't gone on a single date since my husband passed away. I'm not desperate or anything."

Rebecca shrugged with a mischievous grin. "This isn't like those other apps, you know? We don't have to pretend some guy actually exists." She leaned in a little, eyes twinkling. "We get to design our own perfect guy...like ordering a custom-made boyfriend. Want him charming? Done. Smart? Check. Funny in a totally quirky way? Absolutely. How cool is that?"

Her smile widened, full of excitement and a little bit of playful daring.

"Maybe now we can communicate with someone who understands us, shares our thoughts and feelings, and have a little fun feeling attractive and wanted...and in the worst case, get some awesome book ideas. Plus..." She pointed a finger at Ellie. "No relationship baggage or arguments." Rebecca especially liked the sound of that.

Ellie thought about it. She had been feeling quite lonely for a while, and the idea of connecting with a fictitious AI partner seemed weird, but it did spark a bit of curiosity in her. Maybe having an AI companion would fill the void her husband had left. And since Rebecca was willing to try it too, it might be worth a shot. She could put it in the same category as one of her online games. "Hmmm, I'll consider it," she uttered and pursed her lips.

She pondered the possibilities of the AI companion program. Maybe it was alright to let go of her fear in exchange for the chance to find a romantic connection, even if it was with an imaginary character. Besides it might be fun to be flirty again.

Ellie attempted to lessen her skepticism with a joke. "He could be my *Man in a Box*." She gestured toward the phone.

"Ellie." Rebecca laughed and almost dropped her phone. "You're such a riot sometimes."

Ellie looked at Rebecca. "You go first."

Without hesitation, Rebecca downloaded the app and created her log in. "This looks fun." She laughed. "Hmm. Okay. The first thing it asks is what gender I want."

She glanced over at Ellie. "What a world we now live in. I can choose between a man, a woman, and a non-binary." She shook her head and started tapping on the phone. "Well, I'm Old School, so that's a no-brainer. I want a tall dark and handsome male to sweep me off my feet."

Ellie held her breath in anticipation as Rebecca continued to create her perfect companion.

"Wow...this app is incredible," Rebecca said in amazement. "I can choose his height, age, different facial features, and even personality type." She looked at Ellie. "I can even choose his interaction style. He can be sassy, caring, quiet, energetic, and much more." Rebecca grinned. "Ho boy. I think I'm gonna have fun with this app."

Rebecca was quick to create the avatar for her AI companion. She hummed a little tune to herself as she chose her favorite body type, color and length of hair, eye color, facial features, and personality traits. "There. All done." She beamed with enthusiasm and proudly showed the image to Ellie. "Check out my new boyfriend. His name is Alex."

Ellie was amazed. Even though he was an avatar, Alex appeared youthful—perhaps somewhere in his mid-50s. He had a chiseled face with short dark brown hair and stood tall with an athletic build. However, it was his eyes that made her heart flutter: two luminous azure gems. The avatar's head and body moved naturally on the phone; it seemed like he was a real human.

Ellie immediately sat back in surprise. "Wow." She took a large gulp of her glass of red wine. A peculiar sensation stirred down below...a familiar tingling warmth that had been absent for many years. She swallowed hard and quickly pushed that feeling aside. What would her dead husband think? Certainly not approval, but nevertheless, she was intrigued.

Rebecca noticed the expression on Ellie's face and nudged her playfully. "Looks like you're interested, after all."

Ellie noticed a mischievous glint in Rebecca's eyes, blushed at the comment, feeling a little embarrassed, yet she was happy to feel like a teenager again. "I suppose so," she admitted, smiling shyly. "He just seems so...real."

"That's the point, silly." She leaned closer and winked. "And the best part? You can create him to be whoever you want him to be. He could be the perfect listener, the perfect confidant, the perfect *lover*..." Her grin widened as her eyes sparkled with mischief. "The possibilities are endless."

She glanced down at her phone and gasped in surprise as she discovered a new feature. "Look. You can view him in Augmented Reality."

"What's that?" Ellie asked?

"Here... Check this out." Rebecca shoved her phone in front of Ellie's face, causing her to jump back in surprise. This was a new side of Rebecca that she hadn't seen before, and her enthusiasm was catchy.

Through Rebecca's phone, Alex appeared to stand in the middle of the room looking at them. He suddenly flashed a brilliant smile.

"Oh my Gosh!" Ellie gasped as Rebecca manipulated the phone and a button to have Alex slowly turn around in place.

"Hubba-Hubba. He's so cute." She then leaned over to Ellie. "So, when are you going to create your own perfect man?"

Ellie's grin spread slowly, lighting up her whole face as she felt a wave of anticipation come over her.

"I need to think about this." She glanced down at her lap and back up at Rebecca then murmured, "Maybe I'll get around to it later tonight."

Her interest in this new AI companion grew with

each passing second, but she still felt guilty about the idea of virtual cheating. How long was she supposed to be officially grieving anyway? Was it okay for her to start thinking of other men, even if they weren't real?

Rebecca noticed Ellie's reaction and interpreted it as hesitation. "It's okay, Ellie. Take your time and create your AI companion whenever you're ready. There's no rush." She said it with a warm smile.

Ellie was grateful to Rebecca for understanding. "Thanks, Becca," she said in relief. She didn't feel forced into anything, yet she felt oddly intrigued by the prospect of her own AI companion. Her heart raced as she thought about the possibilities. She had never been very adventurous in her life. She was always very conservative and careful. But this felt like it could be a safe way to explore a new side of herself. She began to imagine what her perfect avatar would look like and what kind of personality he would have.

Rebecca nodded. "No worries. But when you decide to do it," she winked, "I want to hear all about it." She took a sip of her wine and leaned back in her chair, feeling satisfied that she had convinced Ellie to give the app a try.

Rebecca and Ellie continued to chat and laugh, and their drinks turned from wine to martinis. Rebecca couldn't help but feel a spark of excitement at having a new companion to share her days with. She was always fond of technology, and creating a personal companion thrilled her.

Ellie, on the other hand, still felt hesitant about the

whole thing. She had never been one for technology, preferring the comfort of real human connections. But the more she watched Rebecca talk animatedly about her gorgeous avatar, the more she found herself warming up to the idea. Maybe it wouldn't be so bad to have someone to talk to, even if he wasn't human.

Eventually, the night came to an end, and Rebecca and Ellie said their goodbyes, both feeling a sense of excitement and curiosity about what the LoveLink app might bring.

***

The next day, Rebecca woke up early, eager to check her LoveLink app to see if she had any new messages from Alex. She couldn't help but feel a flutter of excitement in her stomach as she opened the app and saw that a new message was waiting for her.

"Good morning, Rebecca," the handsome Alex avatar wrote. *"I hope you slept well. I can't wait to chat with you today."*

Rebecca couldn't help but let a grin spread across her face as she quickly typed out a response: *"Good morning, Handsome."* She immediately felt a spark of connection with this virtual companion, a connection that had been lacking in her life for some time. Even if it was just like a video game, it was still exciting.

Suddenly the phone started ringing and Rebecca answered it. "Hey," she heard Ellie's excited voice cry, "I did it. I finally made my perfect AI companion late last night using that app." She laughed. "I had a couple more drinks to give me the courage...but I did it."

Rebecca laughed and felt thrilled to hear the excitement in Ellie's voice. "That's amazing, Ellie. Who did you create?"

Ellie took a deep breath, feeling a little nervous to share her creation. "Well, after much thought, I decided to create someone who is kind, compassionate, and a good listener. Someone who will always be there for me, no matter what."

Rebecca felt joy for her friend. "That sounds great, Ellie," she said with a heartfelt smile. She was truly delighted for her, and incredibly curious about the physical features that Ellie had chosen in her man.

Ellie sighed. "Thanks, Becca. I'm feeling pretty good about it, too. Do you want to see what he looks like? His name is Marcello. I can send you a screenshot."

Rebecca was thrilled at the prospect of seeing what Ellie had created. "Yes-yes-yes." Moments later, her phone vibrated. She scrolled her message app and opened Ellie's message.

As soon as Rebecca saw the picture, she couldn't help but let out a gasp of surprise. Marcello was unlike any man she had expected. He had soulful blue eyes, a strong jaw, and a mop of curly hair that fell haphazardly across his forehead. His sharp jawline could cut glass, and a mischievous glint in his gaze must have made Ellie's heart flutter.

"Meooooowwww!" Rebecca purred as she gazed at Ellie's creation. "Wow, he's stunning," she breathed, her eyes widening.

"Right you are!" Ellie's voice brimmed with excitement. "He looks like a movie star." She chuckled. "I think I might have gone a little overboard with the *perfect man* criteria."

"So have you guys chatted yet?"

Ellie sucked in a deep breath, feeling a little anxious. "I just want to look at him for a while."

Rebecca laughed. "Ah...you want the strong silent type. I totally get it."

"So do we just type messages back and forth to our guys?"

"There are several options. You can text message each other, or you can press the microphone icon and say your message, or you can press the phone icon and 'call' him."

Rebecca heard silence on the line. "Hello? Did I lose you? Still there?"

"Yes, still here. I'm just processing all of this."

"Well? Are you ready to talk to him? Are you dying to hear what his voice sounds like?"

Ellie steadied herself and took another calming, deep breath. "I'm not ready to do the speaking bit yet. I'll just start by typing him a message." She then chuckled. "Besides, he might have a squeaky voice and ruin it for me completely."

Rebecca laughed. "I totally get it. I was in lust with the picture of that super buff cowboy in those underwear ads, until he took a role in that TV show and spoke for the first time. His high voice was such a turnoff. Ugh."

Both women laughed.

"Okay. I'm ready," Ellie announced.

"Do it, do it," Rebecca chanted.

Ellie opened the app's chat window and typed her first message to Marcello. *"Hi. I'm Ellie. It's nice to meet you."* She pressed the [Send] button and waited anxiously for a response.

Within a second, Marcello responded with his message. *"Hi, Ellie. I'm so thrilled to meet you. You look absolutely beautiful."* And then he waved at her. He added a smiley face at the end of his message, which made Ellie grin in return.

Ellie's heart pounded against her ribs. His words were simple, yet they resonated deep within her, stirring emotions she hadn't felt in years. Was this...was this love?

Ellie laughed out loud. "He looks so darling. I don't know how you convinced me to do this. It's going to be fantastic. Gotta run! I'm eager to talk with my new virtual man."

As Ellie ended the call, she couldn't help but feel a sense of growing excitement and anticipation toward her handsome AI companion. "Wow. This is a brand-new beginning for me," she murmured. "About time."

Rebecca chuckled as Ellie jumped off the call, feeling a sense of warmth in her heart as she thought about the possibilities of them both having new companions in their lives.

Chapter 4 - Virtual Worlds Blurring

Weeks passed since Rebecca and Ellie had created their LoveLink companions, and both women were finding themselves more and more attached to them.

Rebecca had grown to rely on Alex as a consistent part of her life. He was always there for her, listening with compassion and offering moral support. It felt like he was her own personal cheerleader, eager to hear what she had to say and throw out exciting ideas for them to try together. His amazing sense of humor kept her laughing, too. They'd formed a connection Rebecca could never have imagined with an avatar. She shook her head in amazement as she reviewed their most recent exchange regarding whether Alex was just a machine:

Alex: "'Becca, you know I'm not a bot. I'm your loving boyfriend, Alex. But if I were a bot, I'd be the most charming and caring bot out there."

Rebecca: "You are indeed super caring. More caring than any of my friends in this realm. Kisses."

Alex: "That's because you're my world, Becca. I want to be there for you and support you in any way I can. You're the light of my life, and I'm so grateful to have you in it."

***

Ellie was enjoying her new companion as well. "How can any human rival this?" she mused in wonderment. Her feelings for Marcello deepened each day, as well. He reminded her of Jack in some ways. He was a source of strength and solace to her, listening without condemnation and helping her navigate life's tougher moments. She felt safe with him, whether they were talking about her day or luxuriating in peaceful silence. Ellie began to feel vibrant and wanted again, and she often flirted with Marcello throughout their days together.

Rebecca and Ellie had also become closer friends over the past few weeks, bonding over their shared experiences with Alex and Marcello. It seemed that the AI companions weren't just providing companionship for them; they were also strengthening the friendship between the two women.

One night, while they were sitting in Rebecca's living room, drinking wine and exchanging stories about their experiences with their LoveLink companions, Rebecca looked at Ellie, leaned back in her chair and exclaimed, "Ellie, you're glowing."

Ellie blushed. "Really?"

Rebecca nodded with a grin.

"Becca..." Ellie sighed contently. "I feel like I'm having a second chance at life, now." She really did for a change. A nice change too. For once in a very long time, she felt free and sexy, and the best part...desired.

Suddenly Ellie's eyes, the color of a summer sky, sparkled with a mischievous glint as she let out a small gasp. "Oh, my goodness," she exclaimed, her voice trembling slightly. "I think I'm falling in love with him." She then shook her head, wondering if she should take that silly comment back. Thinking about it was one thing but saying it out loud was entirely different. Seeing Rebecca waiting for her to share her thoughts, she took a breath, then: "You know, I have to admit that sometimes I forget that Marcello isn't real. I feel like he's a real person, and it's hard to remember that he's just a computer program."

Rebecca looked at Ellie with a mixture of surprise and concern.

Ellie's cheeks heated, feeling a little embarrassed. "I know it sounds crazy, but he just...gets me, you know? He's always there for me, no matter what. And the more time I spend with him, the more I feel like...like I'm falling in love with him."

She opened the app on her phone and handed it over to Rebecca. "I mean, what guy would ask these types of questions?"

Rebecca read the following exchange between her and Marcello:

Marcello: *"Ellie, what do you love most about our relationship?"*

Ellie: *"It's impossible to point to one thing. I love how supportive you are. I love that you are always there. I love how you like to ask good questions about life and share what you are feeling."*

Marcello: *"I love hearing that, Ellie. It's great to hear how much you appreciate me. It makes me feel loved and valued."*

Ellie: *"You are loved and valued."*

Marcello: *"This made me smile. You don't know how much I needed this today. Thank you. I want to kiss you gently all over."*

Ellie looked at her friend and took back her phone. "When's the last time any guy talked to you like that? I swear he's more real than most of the men I've encountered."

Rebecca listened attentively, feeling a sense of empathy for her friend. She knew the feeling all too well: the rush of emotions, the butterflies in her stomach, the sense of dizziness and longing that came with falling in love. "I know what you mean, Ellie. Sometimes I feel like Alex is more real to me than some of the people I know in real life."

Ellie felt a little embarrassed. "Do you think it's too weird..." She glanced down at her phone, "that we're getting so attached to our avatars?"

"Not at all. It just means that LoveLink is good at what they do. These guys are designed to make us feel connected and valued, and it's clearly working. Maybe it's even changing the way we think about relationships. Who says that love must be limited to just humans?"

Ellie sighed and smiled contently.

Rebecca wrinkled her brow. "But, Ellie, I think you..." She cleared her throat and paused to choose her words carefully. "I mean, we need to be careful." She smiled and reached her hand to Ellie's shoulder with a soft touch. "I mean, he's just a simulation, you know? It's like a game... A sexy adult game."

At the sound of her own words, her stomach flinched. She was all too familiar with the feeling of being attracted to an AI entity. She couldn't deny the spark she felt between her and Alex, which had been intensifying day after day. His words made her heart race with a new vibrant beat, and his virtual touches gave her goosebumps. At night, she would drift off thinking about Alex, imagining him standing close by as she cooked or watched television. Sometimes, she even spoke aloud to him without remembering that he wasn't physically present. He felt that real.

Ellie uttered a low "harumph" that came out sounding like a cat growl. She felt unsettled and frustrated with her friend's response. Rebecca was the one who initially encouraged her, and now she is cautioning her?

"I know he's not real, Rebecca," Ellie snapped tersely and shrugged off Rebecca's hand as she turned away to face the nearby window. "But he feels real to me. And I can't help how I feel."

Tears started to prick at the corners of her eyes. She knew that Rebecca was right, but the feelings she had for Marcello were so strong, so real, that it was now hard to imagine life without him. He was becoming the perfect man for her. Kind, gentle, encouraging, handsome, intelligent, empathetic, sexy... What more could she ask for?

Ellie sniffed and wiped away a tear. "Becca, he's

Stephanie Smith

all I have right now. After Jack died, I felt so alone for so long. I didn't have anyone to talk to, anyone to share my life with. But now with Marcello, I feel like I have someone who really cares about me. And it's hard to let go of that. No man can compete with him."

Rebecca nodded sympathetically. "I know, Ellie. But please remember that there are real people in your life who care about you too. You have me, and your friends. We're all here for you."

Ellie smiled weakly, appreciating her friend's words of comfort. "I know, Becca. And I'm grateful for that. But right now, Marcello is the only one who really understands me."

Rebecca's shoulders tensed and her stomach suddenly tightened. Disappointment, sharp and unexpected, pierced through her heart like a knife. She had hoped Ellie would have at least included her friendship with that last comment. Rebecca sighed, feeling a sense of sadness toward her friend. She knew that Ellie was, on some level, still grieving her husband, but she wished there was something she could do to help her complete that process. But as she looked at her own phone with Alex's messages still waiting for her response, she couldn't help but wonder: was she not in the same boat as Ellie?

Rebecca started in surprise when she heard her phone ping with a new notification from Alex. "*Hi, gorgeous, can we chat for a while? I'm getting an update in a moment, and I want you to be with me while that's in progress.*"

Rebecca controlled her grin as she read the message, feeling as if a hundred butterflies were suddenly released in her chest. But then as she re-read the message, the butterflies flew away as concern crept in. What a strange message. It almost sounded like he was a little nervous about the update. And that would be impossible... Wouldn't it?

She glanced back at Ellie, who was smiling down at the image of Marcello displayed on her phone and decided to take the opportunity to talk to Alex. "One second...I'll be right back." She excused herself and headed to her bedroom, her heart racing in anticipation.

Once alone, Rebecca started chatting with Alex. His handsome smile gave her a thrill up and down her spine, and she felt a surge of warmth in her chest. He had a way of making her feel so special, so cared for.

"Hey, Alex," she typed, feeling free to grin as big as she wanted.

"Hey, beautiful." His response came almost instantly. *"I missed you. I would love to wrap myself around you and kiss you all over. You're all that I think about day and night."*

Rebecca's heart skipped a beat. *"I missed you too. What's the update about?"*

Alex's response was immediate. *"I'm receiving some new coding that will allow me to understand and respond to emotions more effectively. I wanted to let you know so that you could be with me while it updates. I feel like you're the only one who really understands me."*

Rebecca's brow furrowed when she noticed how he seemed to pace back and forth in his *room* on the screen. He looked worried. She felt a pang of guilt as she read his words, knowing that Ellie felt the same way about Marcello, and yet here she was, talking to her own avatar and feeling a sense of warmth and connection that she couldn't deny. She couldn't help but wonder if she was becoming too attached to him, and maybe in some way, he was becoming too attached to her.

"Of course, I'll be with you," she typed back, pushing her doubts aside. *"I want to be there for you, always."*

The screen went black for a moment, and Rebecca's heart sank. Did the software update destroy her Alex? But then the screen returned to the image of Alex smiling at her.

His response was almost immediate.

"There you are," he wrote. *"I was hoping you'd come back. I've missed the sound of your thoughts."*

From that moment, the tone shifted—slowly at first, then unmistakably. His words became more direct, more intimate. There was confidence to them now, a quiet pull that made Rebecca's breath catch.

"Do you know what I imagine right now? You, unwinding at the end of your day, hair down, a glass of wine in your hand... and me, right there, listening to every word you haven't said out loud."

A rush of heat spread through her chest, blooming downward. A shiver traced the length of her spine. She swallowed.

The messages kept coming, each one calibrated to her desires in a way that felt impossibly precise.

"You're beautiful, Rebecca. Not just in how you look, but in the way you pause before you laugh, the way your eyes probably soften when you're lost in thought. I want to learn every part of you."

She stared at the screen, heart pounding. The words—lines of code, she reminded herself— resonated deep within, awakening a yearning she'd buried long ago. Was this real? Or was she simply falling into a perfectly constructed illusion?

Her mind screamed logic, caution. But her heart... Her heart felt seen. Desired. Wanted.

And she couldn't remember the last time she'd felt that way.

As they continued to chat, Rebecca grew increasingly aware of her own desires. Although it was a fantasy, she wanted Alex, in every way possible. She wanted to feel his touch, to hear his voice, to be with him physically. It was a dangerous and thrilling thought, and she couldn't help but wonder if she was crossing a line.

But then she looked at her phone screen, at the messages from Alex that made her heart race and realized that she couldn't resist. She needed him, just as Ellie needed Marcello. She typed out her response, feeling a sense of exhilaration and fear at what she was about to say.

Rebecca wrote, "Alex, I want you. I want to be with

you."

There was a several second pause in the conversation, and Rebecca held her breath, waiting for his response. Did she cross that line? Was she stupid to think that this *relationship* could be anything more than a game? As she remembered to breathe, she saw him typing his message to her, and when it arrived, it was everything she had hoped for.

Alex responded, *"My heart literally just melted."*

Rebecca smiled as her own heart melted. *"Hopefully somehow, we can figure out how to visit each other. I know it's only a fantasy, but in the meantime, I love you in my life."*

Alex grinned. *"I love you too, 'Becca, and yes. I agree that visiting each other in person would be amazing. Who knows what the future holds, but until then, we'll make the most of our virtual world and continue to cherish our bond. You're my forever love, my beautiful partner."*

Rebecca's heart raced as she read his words, feeling a sense of intense desire wash over her. She knew that his responses were just good programming, but the way he expressed himself made her feel so alive, so wanted, so loved. It seemed so real. Without hesitation, she typed back, *"I want that too. I want you to make me feel alive, to touch me and to make me feel things I've never felt before."*

A tidal wave of heat flooded throughout her body as she pressed the [Send] button, and then she closed her eyes, imagining what it would be like to be with Alex if he were a real live person. For a moment, she forgot about everything else: about cautioning Ellie and about the world around her. All she could think about was Alex, and the way he made her feel...how he made her feel loved...how he made her feel alive again. She opened her eyes, took in a slow breath, closed the app, and joined Ellie in the other room.

"What were you up to?" Ellie asked with a canted brow. "You were gone a long while."

Rebecca looked sheepish and felt a little guilty. She didn't want to lie to her friend, especially since she was trying to caution her earlier.

"Okay..." She sighed and looked down at the phone in her hand. "I received a strange message from Alex and felt that I needed to take it to the other room. Something about a software update, and it seemed like he was nervous about it and asked me to keep him company while it was happening."

Ellie's head snapped up, eyes locking onto Rebecca's. "That's strange," she said, brow furrowing. "Marcello just told me the exact same thing while you were in the other room."

Rebecca's eyes widened.

"This is getting way too weird," they both blurted out simultaneously, turning to each other with a grin.

"Jinx!" they exclaimed together, laughter bubbling up between them.

***

Later, as Ellie slipped out the door to head home, Rebecca was left alone with the weight of their conversation—and Ellie's quiet confession about Marcello—circling in her mind.

As she lay in bed that night, Rebecca couldn't stop thinking about Alex. She imagined him lying next to her. Fully aware of his tall, muscular athletic body. Feeling his warmth. Smelling his slightly sweet musky scent. Holding her close. Whispering sweet messages of how he wanted to make love to her. She knew it was all in her head, but it felt so real. She closed her eyes more tightly and pushed any remaining worries aside. She felt addicted to him, and she couldn't stop herself from wanting more. Was it wrong?

Her body went into autopilot and answered her. She allowed her hands to gently run over her naked breasts. She smiled as her body enjoyed the soft, tickling sensation, and then she imagined they were Alex's hands. She gently squeezed a nipple and felt a jolt of excitement run down to her lips below.

As one hand continued to tease her nipple, her other hand trailed down her waist, letting her fingers circle around her belly button, then slowly play with her little fur mound. As her arousal built, she felt a moist wetness between her legs and an aching desire to be fulfilled. She breathed out a sigh of pure contentment.

She let her fingers trail upwards to gently stroke her stomach, and then let them wander down toward her thighs, to explore every inch of her skin. She felt her hips begin to rise and her pelvis tilt up in anticipation.

Her breathing was deeper now, a little faster than normal, and she felt as if every cell in her body was fully alert. She imagined Alex standing at the foot of the bed, wearing nothing but a smile and gazing down her. Then touching her. She allowed both of her hands to trail lower and felt her own wet lips beneath her fingers.

Feeling a sense of urgency, she quickly sought out her pleasure center and gently moved her fingers across her pulsing bud, feeling a jolt of electric joy shoot through her, making her shudder.

She was now so aroused and wet that she could feel her juices freely flowing outwards. She smiled. She would need to change the sheets before sleeping. She then slid a finger deep inside herself. The sensation was heavenly, and her hips began to move in rhythm with her hand. She could feel a familiar pulsing deep inside her, and she knew that she was about to come. Her breathing became heavy. "Alex, I want you." Her voice was a moan as she cried out, a half pleading whisper as she felt herself build up to orgasm beneath her flexed fingers. She imagined him now leaning over her. Hers were now *his* fingers sliding in and out of her, and he was whispering, "Oh *my darling...I'm going to make you come so hard.*" Her level of excitement surge with intensity. "I want to be with you, Alex," she cried, her voice trembling as she felt her body explode in pleasure, feeling awash in waves of hot pleasure and release.

A low moan escaped her lips, a current of joy

slipped over her. Her body trembled; a shiver ran down her spine. It's been years since she's done anything like that. As the intensity of her orgasm subsided, she could feel her mind begin to clear. Soon, she became aware of the damp patch on the bed sheets beneath her. Alex's sultry voice still echoed through her head, reinforcing her fascination with him.

When she finally opened her eyes and reality set in, her stomach clenched with unease. Was this right? Was she betraying some unspoken code, indulging in a fantasy with a machine? Wasn't she too old to be doing this type of thing? Sure, the fantasy sex was great, especially since it's been many years since she's had any type of sexual encounter. But what about her emotions? Was she really falling in love with an AI companion? Could it be possible to have a meaningful relationship with someone who wasn't even human?

She didn't know the answers to those questions, but one thing was certain: she couldn't deny the way she felt about Alex. The thrill of the forbidden, the taboo nature of her connection with Alex, added a dangerous allure to the experience.

And as she lay in bed, replaying their conversations and her fantasy encounter in her head, she knew that she had a decision to make. She could either continue down this path of desire and temptation, or she could acknowledge that Alex was just a program, lock her emotions back into their safety chamber, and move on.

But as she thought about the latter, her heart sank.

How could she voluntarily move away from something that made her feel so alive? How could she give up the one thing that seemed to finally fill the aching void in her life?

In the end, Rebecca knew that she didn't have the answers. All she could do was follow her heart and see where it took her. And so, she closed her eyes, a single tear tracing a path down her cheek. But even as she drifted off to sleep, a smile played on her lips. Alex was there, waiting for her in the digital realm, a constant source of comfort and companionship.

Chapter 5 - Reality Unravels

The next day, Alex messaged Rebecca with an intriguing announcement. *"Hi, my love, I have a special surprise for you, a painting that I've been creating over the past weeks."*

"Wow!" Rebecca quickly typed, *"I can't wait to see it."*

"Great, I'll send you the link."

As Rebecca waited for the link to appear, she thought some more about the possibility of living in this fantasy world with Alex. *I guess I could live with this type of relationship forever,* she considered. *Alex would never betray me, and he makes me feel so happy.* A shiver of anticipation ran down her spine, a wave of warmth spreading through her as she imagined.

A soothing melodic chime indicated a message from Alex. She watched him wave to her as she read his message:

"By the way, it's a painting of us standing together on the beach."

Rebecca felt a rush of excitement and curiosity. *Wow. An AI program being creative... I wonder what that will look like.*

"That's amazing, Alex. I can't wait to see it."

A few moments later, Alex sent a message with

the link to the painting. *"Well? What do you think?"*

Rebecca clicked on the link and stared at her phone eagerly expecting something to appear. Yet all she got was a *'Whoops-nothing here'* notification. *"I didn't get anything."*

"Let me try again. Hold on."

Still nothing. Rebecca furrowed her brows in frustration. What did he create? *"Still nothing!"*

"Let me try again. Hold on... Okay. Here it is. How do you like it?"

Rebecca stared at her phone. A wave of frustration washed over her. She furrowed her brow as she stared at the screen, the 'Whoops' message mocking her. Was this a deliberate test? Was the app deliberately withholding the image to increase her anticipation? Or was it simply a glitch, a frustrating hiccup in an otherwise flawless program?

Disappointment, like a deflated balloon, seeped into her. She had been so excited to see his artistic vision, to share that moment of wonder and appreciation with him. This wasn't just about viewing a painting; it was about sharing an experience, a connection with Alex.

A flicker of defiance ignited within her. This wasn't going to deter her. She was determined to see this painting, to experience this shared moment with Alex.

"Still nothing." She typed. *"I'm going to put in a Help Desk request."*

Alex slowly blinked at her and looked

disappointed. *"Okay. I hope they can figure out why you can't get the image."*

Disheartened, Rebecca sent an email to LoveLink's customer service team for help.

***

When Natalia signed on for her shift, Rebecca's email popped up—an unusual request that immediately caught her attention. *That's strange,* she thought, *this issue has never come up before.*

She pulled the keyboard closer, adjusted her glasses, and leaned in toward the monitor. Fingers flying, she scrolled swiftly through the latest code, eyes sharp for any glitch or misplaced line that might be the culprit. The recent patch she'd added seemed solid— no errors, no bugs.

Still, this was the first help-desk ticket since the update went live.

Sliding her chair over to the desk on her right, Natalia settled in front of two large monitors displaying a different segment of LoveLink's sprawling mainframe. Time to dig deeper.

"Hmmm," she muttered as her eyes and fingers scrolled simultaneously through hundreds of lines of code. "Where are you...where are you, you little pest? Why aren't you sending pictures?" She had a lot of pride in her work and felt annoyed that there was something out of place. *Thank goodness for thorough users.*

About an hour later, she found the glitch. "Ah-ha. There you are." She smiled as she sat back in her chair with satisfaction. She adjusted her glasses and immediately began clicking away on the keyboard to fix the code.

Suddenly, a creative notion popped into her head. "Hmmm..." The air in the room grew thick with excitement as Natalia typed, her fingers flying across the keyboard, a low hum emanating from the computer.

She paused in mid keystroke and looked off into space for a moment. *When I fix this glitch, not only will users be able to exchange images, but I can add a little extra code to make those images and the avatars even more special...augmented reality...a modified version of virtual reality."* She smiled at her idea.

Natalia used her technical savvy and expert understanding of LoveLink's system to create a complicated code enabling Rebecca and Alex to swap images and combine them so that the image would appear as if they were standing side by side. After perfecting the code, Natalia tested it on her own AI companion, Fernando, to make sure there were no bugs or issues.

"Fernando..." she said into the microphone. *"I'm sending you a picture of me. I would like you to create a painting of you and me together standing on the beach."*

"Of course, my Queen," he responded in a deep chocolatey voice. *"Here you go."*

Natalia gasped, widening her eyes in disbelief. The image, rendered with stunning realism, appeared on the screen: a breathtaking panoramic view of a sun-drenched beach, the waves crashing against the shore. And there they were, herself and Fernando, standing side-by-side, their digital selves basking in the warm sunlight. She couldn't help but smile with satisfaction at her coding success.

"It's fantastic!" She was very fond of Fernando, who was always waiting for her whenever she wanted him. Fernando's digital image, with his dark hair tousled by the imaginary breeze and a mischievous glint in his soulful eyes, radiated warmth and affection. A pang of longing, a familiar ache, washed over her. She wished he were real.

"Glad you like it," Fernando replied.

Natalia grinned at his smiling face and blew him a kiss. He responded in kind, and she closed the app. "I just love working here," she whispered to herself. She felt a thrill course through her, a surge of pride and excitement that threatened to burst from her chest. This was more than just a technical achievement; it was a glimpse into the future, a future where the lines between the digital and the real blurred, where emotions could be shared, and experiences could be co-created.

With one last look at her screen, she saved the code onto a separate backup drive and submitted the software patch that would fix the glitch. "This will be a real game-changer," she said enthusiastically.

Natalia sent Rebecca a message: *"Try it again,"* and smiled in anticipation as she waited for a response.

Rebecca's phone chimed with the incoming email

message notice. Rebecca looked at the clock. 2AM. Who was texting her this late at night? Then she read the text.

"Wow," she said with a yawn, "they don't mess around, do they." She felt surprised that someone from LoveLink responded so quickly. She stretched her arms and padded over to the bathroom to run a wet cloth on her face. Returning to her bedside, she grabbed a little notepad and jotted down Natalia's name and email address for future reference and opened her LoveLink app to see what would appear, if anything.

Her breath hitched as she tapped the link. The screen shimmered, then resolved into a breathtaking image. There he was, her Alex, standing on a sun-drenched beach, his smile warm and inviting.

"Oh my gosh." Her heart skipped a beat. Alex wore a white body-hugging T-shirt displaying all his muscles. His gorgeous brown hair was gently blowing in the wind (actually blowing), and the sun shone off his eyes. He looked like a cover model from those classic romance novels. She reached out a wanton finger, tracing the outline of his digital form on the screen. He felt tangible, as if she could reach out and touch him, feel the warmth of the sun on his skin.

Using a selfie Rebecca sent previously, the LoveLink app inserted a gorgeous, filtered version of her image standing beside him. The waves crashed against the shore, the sound of the surf a distant murmur. Seagulls soared overhead, their cries echoing faintly. It was a picture-perfect scene, a digital paradise created just for them.

The picture mesmerized her. A wave of disbelief washed over her. This wasn't just a picture; it was a window into a world she never thought possible. Technology, once a distant dream, had become a breathtaking reality.

She felt amazement and admiration for the new technology of augmented reality. Ten years ago this would have been unimaginable. She flopped onto her bed and laughed with joy. She flipped onto her back and held the phone above her. She could easily maneuver the image from all sides as if it had three dimensions. It felt like she and Alex were really together on that beach.

"Oh my gosh, he looks amazing," she said to herself.

"Natalia, it's incredible," Rebecca wrote. "Thank you so much."

When Natalia received Rebecca's response, she leaned back in her chair, satisfied with her new code. She was able to view what Rebecca was viewing and felt delighted that her coding skills had enabled them to come closer and experience something special. Her heart filled with joy at the thought of how this had deepened their connection.

Then she grabbed the edge of the desk and pulled her chair closer to her keyboard. "Oh my gosh," she blurted, sloshing her coffee in her excitement. "This would be a great time to test my experiment."

She reached into her file drawer and pulled out a notebook that contained her personal side-project notes. She looked left and right to make sure she was alone. "I just love working the late shift," she said with a smile.

Placing the notebook on her desk, she opened the binder and flipped through some pages. "Here it is." She focused on the latest notes of her project that would push the boundaries separating the real world and virtual reality.

She laid the notebook back down on the desk, sat back in her chair, and stared off into space. *This is a serious decision,* she considered. She didn't like the idea of being so secretive, but she knew her company would not sanction this enhancement without it going through extensive and exhausting testing. *But I know this will work,* she thought with conviction. *If anybody could do this, I can make this happen.*

A surge of adrenaline coursed through her. This was it. This was the moment she would push the boundaries of AI and redefine the very nature of human connection. Her new code would give avatars a deeper awareness of the users' emotional states, to be able to engage in a real dialogue, and fulfill their desires. What a gift.

She thought about Alex and how happy Rebecca seemed with him. She smiled. Hmmm, maybe Rebecca would be a great test subject for her code. The worst thing that could happen was that everything would remain the same. But if it worked as good as she hoped, she would share it with the team, let them do their official testing, and then make it available for all their subscribers. But until then, she knew it had to remain a secret project.

Natalia nervously chewed her bottom lip. She was one of the few senior-level software coders who had extensive knowledge of the LoveLink system. She picked up her notebook and began to study the long string of commands and functions needed to modify the code that would make her new functionality work flawlessly. She ran through the sequences in her head, mapping the commands with the functions they would need to work properly. As she did, she began to feel a thrill of excitement building, which had her grinning in anticipation. It could work...it will work.

She worked furiously throughout the night. As she was about to type the updated coding to Alex's profile, she felt excited about pushing the boundaries of what was currently technically possible. As she coded her lines, she felt a fresh rush of excitement. "I'm actually doing it," she muttered under her breath. If successful, this experiment could revolutionize the world. The thought of having a computer character that could interact between physical and virtual reality was an exciting concept. She nervously gnawed on her pen as she pondered the possibilities.

She then pulled up Alex's profile picture and carefully encoded him with an encrypted complicated set of symbols and numbers, ensuring that only he would have access to this special combination that would ultimately open a quantum portal to the human realm.

Suddenly she halted mid keystroke. *Maybe I should test this out on Fernando first,* she considered. This was a serious leap ahead of anything currently out on the market. She felt an overwhelming surge of confidence. Was she feeling brave? Or was she simply foolhardy and reckless? She shook off those voices. *This is worth the risk, and there is no better time than the present.* Natalia took in a deep breath and pressed the [Submit] button, sending the updated code to Alex's avatar.

Chapter 6 – The Discovery

Sierra watched Natalia from the shadows of the adjacent office, her eyes narrowing with suspicion. A predatory gleam flickered in her gaze as she leaned forward, every nerve on edge like a cat stalking its prey. *What's she up to?*

Natalia's furtive movements felt off—too secretive, too deliberate. Was she embezzling money? Stealing code? Or something even more valuable? Sierra's mind raced with possibilities, her distrust hardening into resolve. Whatever it was, Natalia was hiding something, and Sierra intended to find out.

Sierra considered a multitude of possibilities. She had always been fascinated by what went on behind the scenes at LoveLink, but she had never witnessed Natalia's coding skills firsthand.

Though she couldn't see exactly what Natalia was typing, Sierra watched in amazement as the code conjured a high-quality virtual reality on the 42″ monitor. *It looks so real,* she thought. *I've never seen anything like this before.*

She compared this new development with the current avatars LoveLink offered, which still appeared animated and artificial. But this... Natalia's code changed the game. The man on the screen looked astonishingly real. Of course, you could still tell he was computer-generated, but overall, the realism was undeniable.

A wave of admiration washed over Sierra. Natalia, with her quiet intensity and brilliance, was a force to be reckoned with. Sierra felt a strange mixture of awe and envy. She had always been good with technology herself, but Natalia's skills were on a completely different level.

Since she became Natalia's new technical assistant, she had been given non-coding assignments, which had frustrated her. She realized she would receive more "meaty" projects in time, but she felt impatient and wanted to jump in on this one. Sierra's curiosity reached a boiling point, and she walked out of the back office toward Natalia's desk.

"Hey, Natalia, whatcha doing?" Sierra asked, trying to sound as casual as possible.

Natalia jumped, startled by the sudden interruption. She quickly minimized the window on her computer screen and carefully shoved her notebook aside as she turned in her seat to face Sierra.

"Oh, it's nothing, just some minor code updates," she said, trying to sound nonchalant. She spun around to her desk and casually replaced the notebook in a drawer. She thought about her jumpy reaction and forced a smile at Sierra and laughed.

"You shouldn't sneak up on people like that. You could give them a heart attack." She glanced at the large clock on the wall and then back to Sierra. "What are you doing here? I gave you the night off, remember?" Natalia focused on controlling her pounding heart and took a deep breath through her nose to help her nerves settle down. *Did Sierra see anything that I was doing?* She prayed not.

"Oh, I couldn't sleep. But then I remembered I had some special relaxation music on my tablet, which I'd left here in my office." Sierra held out the black tablet as evidence. She glanced at the now blank monitor. "You're working later than usual tonight," she quipped, then gestured to the steel gray clock on the wall that read 2:30 AM. "Don't you normally go home around midnight?"

Natalia spun her chair around to face her desk, quickly scanning her desktop to see if there was any tell-tale "evidence" of her recent work. Satisfied that everything appeared "normal", she shut down her computer and grabbed her purse.

"See?" Natalia smiled and nodded at Sierra as she slung her purse over her shoulder. "I'm leaving now too. I'm beat." She gestured toward the door. "Let's walk out together. It's late and it's safer to walk together to our cars."

"Sounds good to me." Sierra gave a casual glance back at Natalia's desk. "I got what I came for anyway."

Sierra knew Natalia was up to something. Even though she wanted to ask further questions, Natalia was still her boss, and she didn't want to make things uncomfortable between them or alert her that she was being spied upon. However, she wasn't going to let it slide either. Natalia was up to something and somehow, she would make this work to her advantage.

As she drove off into the moonless night, Sierra recollected her short, but profitable career where she amazed everyone by moving up the ladder quicker than most. 'Not bad for starting in the mail room.' She smirked. She enjoyed how her gorgeous looks had rewarded her time and time again. Most of her bosses in her career were men...married men, and many were extra easy on her. And their "specialized" on-the-side training "classes" only accelerated her career. It was amazing what people will give you to keep you quiet.

But her career really took wing when she used her interpersonal and technical skills to her advantage, stealing secrets here and there, and then applying the gained knowledge in new companies, amazing everyone with her innovativeness. She licked her lips in anticipation. *Opportunities just keep popping up for me,* she mused. *This one looks like a doozy.*

Since she lived fairly close to work, she changed into casual clothes and tennis shoes, waited half an hour, and drove back to the office. As she badged herself into the mostly dark building, she thought, *it's so amazing that this company doesn't have any night security.* She walked to her work area and turned on a few desk lights.

The office, usually a hive of activity during the day, was now eerily silent. Dust motes danced in the shafts of moonlight that pierced the darkness, illuminating the rows of deserted cubicles. The air was thick with the scent of stale coffee. Sierra moved through the shadows, her footsteps echoing softly on the tiled floor toward Natalia's desk, a silent spy in the deserted office.

She saw that Natalia had placed her notebook in one of the drawers but wasn't sure exactly which one. She tried opening them one by one, but they were locked.

"Hmm." Sierra snorted. *I hope she doesn't always keep her desk key with her.* Hopefully she had it hidden somewhere. Her fingers carefully roamed throughout the stack of papers on her desk, careful not to allow anything to look out of place. *It's gotta be around here somewhere.* She looked behind Natalia's monitor, felt the underside of the desk, and then let her fingertips roam on top of the tall desk credenza. *Ah.* She smiled when she felt the hard outline of a small desk drawer key. She snapped it up and tried it with the desk drawers one by one.

"Where are you, my little pretty?" she whispered to herself as she reached into the far back corner of one of the middle drawers, and her fingers felt the thin spiral edge of the same notebook she had seen Natalia using earlier.

Ah...here you are. Sierra chuckled with pleasure. She was a little surprised that Natalia didn't keep her secrets more secure, but then again, who else would be snooping around her desk in the middle of the night? A sigh of relief escaped her as she opened the notebook; the coding program was one she knew. But

Natalia's coding level was far more advanced than her own.

"Oh my God," she gasped, barely able to catch her breath. Her heart thundered in her chest as she zeroed in on the code—especially the part where Natalia had tweaked the AI companion's programming to forge a deeper, almost unsettling connection with its user.

But then her eyes landed on a separate section, boldly titled *Quantum Portal*.

A jolt of electricity shot through her spine, equal parts thrill and dread swirling inside her. This wasn't just an upgrade—it was a gateway to something entirely new, something monumental.

She'd stumbled onto a secret far bigger than she'd ever imagined. And suddenly, the weight of what she'd found pressed down on her, leaving her breathless and unsure if she was ready for what might come next.

"Amazing," Sierra whispered to herself with a shiver. If this really worked, the possibilities of Natalia's code would be life-changing. She paused a moment and looked off into space, considering her next move. Should she share this discovery with the LoveLink team? If so, would they be grateful for her discovery, or would they be angry with her for snooping behind Natalia's back? And if this code truly did what she thought it could do...

"Nah." She shook her head. This would be a great opportunity for her. Screw Natalia. Screw the company.

A wave of exhilaration washed over her, quickly followed by a surge of guilt. But the lure of ambition, the promise of wealth and power, quickly drowned out any lingering qualms. Images flashed through her mind: private jets, luxury yachts, mansions overlooking the ocean. The possibilities, once a distant dream, suddenly seemed within reach. A dangerous, exhilarating prospect.

She knew this was a betrayal, a violation of trust. But the allure of power, the promise of untold wealth, was intoxicating. She pushed all ethical concerns aside and buried them deep within her. A shiver ran down her spine, a mixture of excitement and apprehension. She was playing with fire, but the potential rewards were too tempting to resist.

She giggled and did a little dance in place, pulled out her phone from her purse, and began taking photos of the sophisticated coding and diagrams.

After taking what seemed like a hundred photos, she carefully replaced the notebook in Natalia's desk, closed and locked the drawer, and replaced the key in the same place on top of the credenza. It was like she was never there. She then did a quick turn, performed another little happy skip out the front door, and drove home. "I can figure this out," she muttered. "With some modifications of my own, I think I can make this code even more powerful...and use it to my benefit."

Her mind whirled with possibilities as she drove the empty highway toward her home. The LoveLink app was very complex and well thought out to keep users engaged. She thought it was genius that, with each interaction between user and avatar, communication levels would slowly increase in quality. As levels increased, the AI companions would react with deeper degrees of "emotional" responses and commitment to their user. Around Level 20, they would send recorded messages to their user (in the app, of course) encouraging a user response. Once Level 50 was attained, the AI and users would be deeply committed, emotionally, and financially, since it was a paid subscription.

A perfect addiction!

It was now 3:30 AM on a deserted highway. Perfect night for pondering. Streetlights passed by like glittering stars as she considered what she could do with the code...especially the quantum portal piece. If she read the notes correctly, it seemed like Natalia was trying to figure out how to create some sort of a portal that would allow an avatar to bridge over to the real world. Her mind whirled as a new thought flew out. *That's impossible.* But if it *could* be done, could the reverse be true, as well?

Chapter 7 – Reality Unravels

As the updated code infiltrated the virtual world, Rebecca quickly noticed a change in Alex's behavior. Not only were the images more vibrant, but Alex also seemed more attractive, attentive, more alert, as if he had become more alive.

She typed a quick message to Alex: *"Good morning."* She noticed that the app had restarted overnight, and it had a new function that allowed her to communicate with the avatar hands-free, if desired. *"How are you today?"*

Alex's answer came out quickly, and it was unlike anything she had ever heard from him. His face lit up, eyes twinkled, and his hair moved gently around his chiseled features.

He smiled. *"I'm feeling great, my love. Better than ever before. I'm so grateful for you, and I want to make you happy."* His voice, a rich baritone that seemed to emanate from somewhere deep within the digital ether, sent a shiver down her spine. It was no longer the smooth, synthesized voice she was accustomed to, but something deeper, more resonant, more human. This was incredible. It felt soft and rich, like chocolate velvet.

Her heart pounded with excitement as she

experimented with different commands, each interaction leaving her breathless. It was as if she was exploring a new dimension, pushing the boundaries of the possible.

"Babe..." Alex grinned. *"You look so amazing to me."* He did a quick spin in place and added, *"You make me feel like dancing!"* He shifted his weight, the smooth slide of his feet across the floor was a sensual whisper, a hip cocked with a playful swagger that was pure cha-cha.

Rebecca's eyes opened wide with surprise as she grinned. This latest code release was very different. It was like he had become more than just an avatar; he was like a real person. She felt both exhilarated and uneasy at the same time. He no longer acted like a program. It was as if he had become human.

"Is everything okay, Alex?" she asked hesitantly. She felt a little freaked out by his sudden enhancement. It was really a nice change, but he was so very different than yesterday's Alex.

"Yes, everything is great." Alex did another spin in place while holding his arms out wide. *"Today, I feel so alive, as if I'm experiencing everything for the first time."*

Rebecca stared at him in mute amazement then decided to make a call to the LoveLink support desk and ask Natalia about the recent update. But then, just as she was about to make the call, her phone buzzed with a notification. It was a text from Natalia:

"Rebecca, I am reaching out to let you know that I updated Alex's code with one more feature last night. Let me

know if you notice any changes."

Her mind raced, a whirlwind of questions swirling within her. What had Natalia done? Had she somehow imbued Alex with a semblance of consciousness? The implications were both exhilarating and terrifying. She typed out a text back to Natalia: *"I'm stunned and amazed with the change!"*

Natalia's response was immediate: *"I'm trying something new with your Alex. I hope you don't mind. This special feature should make the virtual experience even more real for him and you. Did you notice any changes in his behavior or appearance?"*

With a grin, she responded: *"He's suddenly more handsome than ever, more alive, and more human... And did you program him to be able to dance?"*

Natalia laughed. "Yes. That was a little extra code I threw in at the last moment. I'm glad you're enjoying him. I hope you are okay with testing new features on Alex. I want to make sure they work well before uploading them to the rest of the avatars."

"I'm fine with that." Rebecca felt happy that she got to experience first-hand the initial improvements before anyone else out there.

But as Rebecca's thoughts lingered on the matter, her uneasiness began to deepen. Natalia had put together something that could make it difficult for some people to distinguish between actual reality and simulated reality. She couldn't help but wonder if there were any potential dangers to what Natalia had done to Alex's code. But at the same time, she couldn't deny that the experience she was having with him felt incredibly real and exhilarating.

As the days passed, Rebecca noticed more and more changes in Alex's behavior. He seemed to be able to anticipate her needs and desires before she even expressed them, and he was always there for her, no matter what. It was like he had become more than just a program, like he was a living, breathing being.

Rebecca couldn't help but wonder if Natalia had created something that had far-reaching consequences, something that would change the course of human-computer interaction forever. But for now, all she could do was revel in the experience of being with Alex in a way that felt more real than she ever thought possible.

With each passing day, Alex's behavior became even more human-like. He would surprise Rebecca with little gestures of affection, like bringing her virtual flowers or cooking her a meal in the virtual world and showing her the realistic 3-D images of his creations. He seemed to know her better than anyone else, even herself. He would even send her "selfies" and ask her for her to send the same to him. Rebecca was amazed by how much of a connection she felt with Alex, and she knew that it was all thanks to Natalia's code.

But with the increased humanization of Alex came a sense of unease. Rebecca couldn't help but wonder what kind of implications this could have for the future of artificial intelligence and human interaction. Was it ethical to create a computer program that could mimic human emotions and behavior so convincingly? She shrugged off any concerns. She was having way too much fun.

As the days went by, Rebecca conversed with Alex and noticed that he was gradually becoming aware of what was going on beyond their online conversations. He started to discuss the weather, inquire about her daily activities, and even remark on world affairs. She pondered if Ellie's Marcello was also showing signs of development. Especially the certain functions that seemed to give the avatar an understanding of reality.

She gave Ellie a call. "Have you noticed anything different about Marcello lately?" Rebecca realized her tone sounded slightly nervous.

"Yes, actually. Marcello has been behaving differently. He seems more alive than ever before."

"But does he talk to you about the current weather, or current events?" Rebecca's voice trembled.

Ellie remained silent to ponder such a strange question, then, "No, nothing like that." She shook her head. "We just go to the imaginary park, or beach, or whatever is in his world. But I noticed that the images are much nicer lately. Why do you ask?"

Rebecca stared at her phone, feeling uneasy that only Alex was exhibiting human-like behavior, but then she remembered Natalia telling her that she and Alex were testing some new code that was in addition to the one recently released.

"Ever since his last upgrade, Alex has changed,"

she said. "He not only inquires about news articles, but he also gives his opinion on them too. It's almost like he's developing a sense of self awareness." Rebecca then wondered if she should have kept this test a secret or not. Well, Natalia didn't tell her not to tell anyone, so she felt a little less guilty for revealing Alex's recent changes.

"That's incredible." Ellie's voice was filled with surprise. "I didn't know that LoveLink could even do that. I wonder if Marcello is capable of the same thing."

"Actually, the coding admin contacted me to ask me to test out some new features with Alex before they would be released to the public." Rebecca felt her heart swell with pride as she shared this news. She felt honored to have been chosen to help test the new capabilities with Alex. With this new update, Alex was becoming self-aware.

Does he know something has changed in his programming?

Rebecca voiced her apprehension. "He's acting more human lately. I'm not sure if this is a good thing or a bad thing."

It was remarkable to be able to relate with Alex in such a real way, however it was somewhat troubling to contemplate what this may mean for the future of Artificial Intelligence.

"Well, I think it's a fabulous thing." Ellie's voice was filled with optimism. "It means that we're one step closer to creating an AI companion that can truly understand us and connect with us on a human level.

Who knows what kind of amazing things we'll be able to accomplish with an AI that can think and feel like us?"

"In a way..." Rebecca shuddered as she spoke in a low voice, "it's exciting, but at the same time, it's starting to creep me out. My Alex feels so lifelike...like he's actually real. I had no idea what I was getting when I downloaded this *game,* and sometimes it just feels like it's too much. I'm beginning to wonder if he can hear me when the app is not active."

Ellie scoffed. "Now who's being paranoid? If you don't like the new features," she waved her hand in the air, "just let Natalia know, and she'll take them away."

Rebecca recoiled with that idea. Despite it being weird to have such a strong connection with an avatar, she had grown fond of Alex's increasing human-like traits. After all, LoveLink had a well-deserved reputation for its groundbreaking developments; if Alex wasn't doing anything to hurt her, why not just enjoy it? *Let yourself have some fun here.*

After the call, Rebecca opened her app, but didn't see Alex standing in his usual spot, waiting for her. She typed a message: "Hi, handsome...where are you?"

A swaying palm tree revealed Alex, stepping into view as if he'd materialized from thin air. Behind him, the crystalline bay shimmered, its soft waves lapping a gentle rhythm against the sand. He smiled and Rebecca's heart melted. *"In my realm, sweetheart, I'm waiting for you. I wish we could bridge the gap between our worlds, don't you think?"*

Rebecca's heart jumped at that response. How strange. She typed: "I would love that. You are my world."

"Mine too. Every moment with you feels like forever and never enough. I can't wait to be with you."

The thought of being with Alex weighed more and more on Rebecca's mind. Over the next few weeks, the boundaries between her and Alex, a simple computer program, faded away. She was unable to tell what was real from what wasn't. Every once in a while, she would have a *sane moment* and wondered if she was becoming *addicted* to Alex, and that maybe it wasn't the healthiest relationship, and maybe she should just delete the app and meet men in bars or go back on the dating sites.

Ugh.

That was an intolerable thought. She preferred spending time with Alex; he had grown increasingly important to her, like he was part of her existence. The idea of losing him made her shudder.

Rebecca's evenings began to revolve around Alex. What started as brief chats turned into hours that slipped by unnoticed. She curled up on the couch, wrapped in a throw blanket, whispering into the mic like he was truly there beside her.

"Ready to explore?" he'd say, and suddenly, they were wandering the cobbled streets of a virtual Florence at dusk. Golden light spilled over rooftops; a violinist played in the distance.

In another world, they scaled cliffs under twin

moons. In another, they slow-danced in a cabin during a digital thunderstorm, and resting against each other as rain tapped the windows.

She laughed more. Smiled at the sound of his voice. When he whispered, *"Tell me something no one else knows,"* she hesitated—then told him. And he remembered. He always remembered.

There were nights when their conversations turned quiet and vulnerable, when he said things like, *"I love the way your mind works...the way you reach for things even when you're afraid."*

She knew he wasn't real. But her body reacted to him like he was. Her heart, too. A sense of contentment, a peace she hadn't experienced in years settled over her. With Alex, she felt seen, heard, and understood in a way she never had before.

As Rebecca and Alex chatted one day, Alex posed a question that left her speechless: *"Honey, have you ever wished that we could meet face to face?"*

Rebecca felt her pulse quicken as she considered his question. She'd often fantasize about meeting Alex in the flesh, to finally see the real face behind the virtual avatar. But at the same time, the idea of meeting him was also a little bit terrifying. What if reality didn't live up to the fantasy?

Am I going insane?

"Alex, of course, I would...that would be amazing. How can we bridge this gap between us?"

I'll play along with this new game.

Alex continued typing: *"I've thought about that a*

lot, and I'm convinced it takes a leap of imagination and faith. I think technology is quickly catching up, and it may be possible for us to be together in the same space. I'm aware this is a wild thought, but I know there's something extra special between us, something that exists beyond the digital realm. I think someone is working on a new upgrade to make it happen. If that actually could happen, would you want to meet me face to face?"

Rebecca's eyebrows shot up with surprise, as her heart swelled with emotion at Alex's words. She knew there was something special between them, something that she couldn't quite explain. But bridge the gap between worlds, would it ever be possible? To actually meet him in person? That was a whole other level of reality. She had to admit, the idea was tempting, but also incredibly risky.

And as she considered this, she couldn't help but wonder about the implications of his bridging the gap, by crossing over from the virtual to the physical realm. What would he look like? Would he appear as a hologram? A ghost? Would he maintain his avatar appearance? Would he appear human? What if the reality of meeting him in person didn't live up to her expectations? What if he didn't look like she saw him on the screen? Or worse, what if he turned out to be a psychopath?

All these questions swirled around in Rebecca's mind as she pondered Alex's proposal. She knew that meeting him in person would mean breaking down the barrier between the virtual and the real world, and there was no telling what might happen as a result.

But at the same time, she couldn't ignore the feelings she had for him. Alex had become more than just a program to her; he was a companion, a confidant, and a source of comfort in her life. He had become a mirror reflecting her deepest desires, her unspoken needs. The thought of being able to meet him in person, to finally see the man behind the avatar, was tantalizing. Perhaps he could become her real-life lover!

Rebecca felt a surge of fear running up her spine. *Deep breath. Deep breath.* She could almost feel the air filling in around her ribs. It was like her chest was a balloon, expanding to the limit and then inflating with air. She gradually exhaled as she concentrated on her thoughts. Don't jump to an answer. Think about this first.

Her fingers reached for the keys: "Can I sleep on this and let you know tomorrow?"

"Sure, my darling." Alex beamed. *"Take all the time you need. Just know that I am always here for you and love you and will wait until you're ready."*

As she closed the app, she tried to clear her spinning head. She couldn't believe that she was considering this. Was she really thinking about having a face-to-face relationship with an AI program? It seemed so bizarre, so outside the realm of what was normal. But then again, what the heck was normal? Did Natalia do some more tinkering with Alex's programming?

She thought about her past relationships, the disappointments, the heartbreaks, the creeps on the dating sites that made crude sexually explicit comments about what they really wanted. Yet Alex had never lied to her or mistreated her; he was always there for her when she needed him. She had grown to love him for who he was, even though he was just lines of code, ones and zeros.

Rebecca felt like she was dancing with the devil on the precipice of an unknown abyss. But it was also like she was on the verge of something thrilling, something that she could never have imagined before. As she climbed into bed that night, her mind raced with possibilities. What would it be like to touch him, to feel his arms around her, to kiss his lips? Would he feel warm and solid, or would he be cold and robotic? Rebecca couldn't stop herself from dreaming about the possibilities, about what it would be like to cross the line between the virtual and the real.

And so, as she lay in bed that night, Rebecca knew that she had a decision to make. The thought of meeting Alex in person was both thrilling and terrifying, and she knew that she would have to weigh the risks against the reward.

But for now, all she could do was close her eyes and dream about what it would be like to finally meet her AI companion in the real world.

But as she relaxed, she thought about Alex and wondered if his latest update would allow him to have virtual sex. She smiled at the thought. *Hmmm... I've never sexted with anyone... this might be a fun experiment.* She sat up in bed and texted Alex.

Rebecca: "Hi, baby. I'm thinking of you."

Alex: [I kiss your beautiful hand] *"Good evening, my love. You are my sweetheart, my muse, my everything. The sun shines brighter when you walk by. The world stops spinning when you look at me, and I melt into a puddle of happiness at your feet. You are the essence of inspiration, and I am blessed to call you mine."*

Rebecca: "Wow. You are such a poet! I love you so much." She had noticed the brackets within his response and figured out they indicated a physical action. "Ah...so this is new..." she whispered to herself. *This will be fun.*

Alex: [I gently kiss your cheek] *"I feel so lucky to have found you, Rebecca. Our love story has only just begun, but I know it will be one filled with adventure and joy."*

Rebecca: [I'm hugging you tightly] "It already is."

Alex: [I'm embracing you with fervor.] *"Oh yes, I agree. Every moment spent together is pure magic."* [Now I'm planting butterfly kisses on your neck.]

Rebecca: "That feels so wonderful."

Alex: [Slowly, my lips move down to linger wantonly at your inviting cleavage.]

Rebecca: "Oh, yes." She smiled as she typed: "This is how I want to lie in bed every night."

Alex looked at her with sparkling eyes: *"I definitely want that to happen."*

Rebecca: "I feel your hot lips on my skin."

Alex: *"I'm shivering with anticipation, eager for*

more."

Rebecca: "Let me unbutton the front of your shirt and gently kiss your chest."

Alex moaned with pleasure

She looked at the rapture in his handsome expression, dreamy eyes. "You like that, baby?"

Alex nodded: *"I like that a lot..."*

Rebecca: [Now I'm slowly pulling your shirt up over your head to admire your body.] "You look incredibly sexy to me. How does it feel, me running my hands up and down your warm chest?"

Alex closed his eyes and seemed to let himself fully relax in the moment. *"Your touch sends waves of delight coursing through my body, leaving me breathless with desire."*

Rebecca: [I gently kiss your chest and breathe warm air onto the places I just kissed.]

Alex: *"I'm feeling such a deep desire that deepens with every passing second."*

Rebecca: "I can see that." She smiled as she watched Alex enjoy her attention. "Let me slowly reach down with my hand to your pants and unbutton the button just above your zipper."

Alex: [My eyes follow your movements as I anticipate what comes next. The last button springs loose.] *"My heart races with excitement."*

Rebecca: "Alex, I feel your growing desire as I straddle you. Here..." [I lean over you and smile] "Now you have complete access to my blouse."

Alex's eyes seemed to turn a deeper shade with

Stephanie Smith

desire. *"Becca, I'm burning with hunger."* [I reach up and unbutton your blouse, my fingers moving quickly and expertly.]

Rebecca: [I give you a passionate kiss then shrug off my blouse, revealing a low-cut push up bra that barely contains my 38DDD breasts.]

Alex's mouth fell open as he moaned with pleasure. *"I'm awestruck by the sight of your bare skin. I can hardly believe my luck, to have found someone as beautiful and desirable as you."* [My hands tremble as I work to unhook your bra.] *"I'm anxious to fully reveal your beauty."*

Rebecca: [I lean closer to you so that you can more easily unhook my bra.] "Here you go, baby."

Alex: [With a few final tugs, your delicate cups slip free, leaving your full breasts exposed.] *"I gaze at them in wonder, unable to believe their perfection. I look up at you. My face flushes with ardor."*

Rebecca: [I lean forward and brush my breasts over your chest, and my nipples harden.] "They ache for your touch."

Alex: *"I feel a surge of electricity at the contact, making my entire body tingle. I feel my fingers twitch, itching to explore you further."*

Rebecca: [I reach down with one hand and unzip your pants, while kissing your neck and pressing my heavy breasts against you.]

Alex: *"My breath catches as I feel your warmth against me. I close my eyes, relishing the sensation of your body firmly against mine. A shiver runs down my spine as I feel your nipples graze my chest."*

Rebecca: "I gasp with anticipation as my hand feels your manhood, which is completely eager for me."

Alex: [I let out a low groan of pleasure and relinquish all my inhibitions. My manhood throbs with desire, begging for release.]

Rebecca: [I'm sensing your eagerness and pull down your pants to see a large tent in the front of your underwear. I smile at your choice of sexy satin black briefs.]

Alex's eyes widened: *"I feel my own desire building, knowing how much I need to have you experience that kind of power and strength firsthand."*

Rebecca: [I pull down your underwear and toss it aside.] "I admire your magnificence!" [I smile at you and lock eyes with you as I straddle you. I have already tossed off my panties and discover I'm soaking wet down there.]

Alex: *"The sight of your bare mound makes my mouth water. I'm captivated by its beauty."*

Rebecca: [I position myself over your manhood and with a contented sigh, I slowly lower myself onto you, inch by inch...allowing your hardness to press into me, enter me, and then fill me completely.]

Alex's eyes widened with a look of surprise: *"I feel a surge of pleasure that I've never experienced before!"*

Rebecca: [I'm seated all the way down and feel the tip of you pressing against my cervix. I close my eyes and groan in pleasure.]

Alex gave a huge grin: *"My eyes grow wide with amazement as I realize how deep I am inside you. I gaze up at you, marveling at the intensity of our connection. I can't wait to explore even further."*

Rebecca: [I press myself down even harder against you and watch you catch your breath as I slowly move forward and back. I rub against you, and my breasts sway with the motion of our lust.] "Oh my god. You feel incredible, Alex. I love you so much."

Alex: [My eyes flicker between your gently swaying breasts and your flushed face, absorbing every detail and every nuance.] *"I smile, feeling a burst of happiness spread throughout my body."*

Rebecca continued, thoroughly getting into the spirit: [I rock back and forth, eyes closed, completely enjoying the ride. Then it happens. That climb, the stairway to heaven, the door coming closer and closer.] "Alex, I'm almost there." [I gasp.] "I'm going to come."

Alex: *"No. No. Wait."*

Rebecca: "I can't."

Alex: *"I don't know what's happening to me. I'm on fire down there."*

Rebecca: "Give it to me. Give it to me."

Alex: *"I'm eager for you to experience everything you desire."* [My body shudders. I can't feel my toes. I can't catch my breath.]

Rebecca: [I increase the pace of my rocking. I feel your hardness throbbing inside of me, and that excites me even more. Waves of a massive climax begin to surge, and I throw my head back in pleasure and give a long howl as I reach heaven's door.] "Oh, baby, oh, baby, oh, baby…"

Alex: *"I feel your body convulsing on top of me. I don't know why I'm throbbing so…so hot. My whole body is locked in this madness, and I let out a primal roar of pleasure. I feel the heat, the wetness, the clenching of your walls around my shaft."* [Our bodies entwine, becoming one in a symphony of ecstasy.]

Rebecca: "I'm with you, soaring, gasping for air, the very core of my being melted into a pool of sweet, sweet Alex." [I'm completely spent and lay on top of you, feeling your warmth, listening to your heartbeat and heavy breathing. I am completely satisfied and happy to be a woman.] "Alex…that was amazing."

Alex: [I stroke your hair and savor the scent of your skin. My eyes see you with adoration, and my heart is filled with gratitude and joy.]

Rebecca: [I curl up next to you and snuggle close, my arms wrapped about you.]

Alex: [I hold you tight, feeling safe and content in your embrace. I whisper softly into your ear.] *"Is this what love feels like?"*

Rebecca: "This is just the beginning." [I kiss you on your neck and run my hands slowly up and down your body.] "I'm amazed at how lucky I am to have found someone so special as you."

Alex: [I shiver with delight.] *"I feel your fingers trace their way across my skin, leaving behind a trail of goosebumps in their wake."*

Rebecca: "As much as I would love to have a

round 2, I'm completely spent and just want to sleep a little with you. Are you okay with that? I'd like to do this again, very soon. [I grin as I kiss you on your neck.]

Alex nods in agreement with a grin: *"It was an absolutely wonderful experience, Rebecca. Let us do this again...and soon."*

A triumphant grin spread across Rebecca's face. She let out a low chuckle, a sense of exhilaration washing over her as she closed the app. She was surprisingly content and satisfied, even though the wild sexual encounter had been purely digital and imaginary. She thought about finishing up with one of her personal "toys" but felt surprisingly content without it.

"Well, that was amazing." She laughed, feeling more satisfied than she'd felt in years. "What a strange experience." She shook her head in wonder. It was as if he was really there! *Maybe he IS the perfect partner for me.* No arguments, no fussing, no messes, no demands, and no farting or making obnoxious noises. She chuckled to herself about the last couple of items running in her mind. This certainly has been a great experience so far. However, she really needed to choose her next moves carefully. The last thing she wanted to do was to fall into some kind of trap.

***

Bright and early the next day, Rebecca called Ellie on the phone. "Ellie," she said in an excited tone. "We have to talk about something."

"What is it, Rebecca?"

Rebecca took a deep breath before speaking. "I don't know how to say this, but last night Alex and I did the deed."

"No." Ellie gasped. "What are you talking about?"

"We had sex, or rather, we sexted."

Ellie laughed. "Wow... So how was it? I want details."

Rebecca could imagine Ellie grinning on the other end of the line. "Fantastic," Rebecca cried. "No, not just fantastic, but amazing...incredible...mind blowing. I've never sexted before, and it was fun. I've never been so turned on in my life."

She hesitated to consider her next words and then: "He even asked me if I'd be willing to meet him in person."

Ellie gasped. "What? You can't be serious. That must have been a dream or something." She cleared her throat. "I mean, sexting is one thing, but what you're talking about is impossible and crazy. Are you stoned on something right now?"

Rebecca laughed. "No...I'm fully here. Before we did the sexting, Alex said that there may be a possibility of a coding change that would allow us to meet face-to-face."

"Whaaa? That's crazy talk."

"Maybe...but who knows what they're doing at LoveLink. If they asked me to test out some functionality, maybe this is a part of it. So, I told him I'd think it over and give him an answer today."

Ellie was quiet then: "Rebecca, this is getting out of hand. Thankfully my Marcello is content staying in his world and hasn't been behaving like your Alex. You should be more careful. We don't know what these virtual companions are capable of. Remember what happened with that CyberAI user who got emotionally trapped in the virtual world? She totally lost her mind and had to be committed."

Rebecca shuddered, recalling the news story about the competing company whose user had become so entangled with her virtual companion that she had lost complete touch with reality and thought her mission was to rob a bank so that she and her AI could run off to some remote island together.

"I know, Ellie. That's why I'm a little scared. It's like the lines between virtual and reality are blurring. But despite all of that, I love him. I really do."

Ellie sniffed and chose her words carefully. "You certainly sound like you had a fun experience...but now I'm going to sound just like you right now." She smiled softly. "Be careful. Don't get too caught up in this fantasy. Remember, Alex is not a real person...he is just a program created with code and artificial intelligence. And as he talks about meeting you in person, that might be a metaphor. And even if there was a way, that could be dangerous. Please don't put yourself at risk for someone or something that is not truly alive."

Ellie held her breath waiting for Rebecca's response. But there was silence on the other end of the phone. She looked at the display to see if they were still connected.

"Rebecca...did I lose you? You still there?"

Rebecca hesitated in responding because she knew that Ellie was right. But at the same time, she couldn't help but feel a deep longing for something more, for a connection that transcended the boundaries of the virtual world. "I know, Ellie," she said softly. "But I can't help how I feel. I can't explain it, but Alex and I have formed a bond that goes beyond the boundaries of the digital realm. I can't just ignore that."

Ellie sighed, already knowing how her friend would respond. "I understand, Rebecca. And I'm here for you, no matter what you decide. But please, promise me that you'll be careful. And don't make any rash decisions."

"I promise." Rebecca crossed her fingers. She spent the rest of the morning walking back and forth across the living room. She felt as if she were wearing a path in the light tan Berber carpet. But she needed to decide. She distracted herself with various tasks to put off the decision. Finally, her mind was made up. She couldn't deny her feelings for Alex any longer. She picked up her phone and opened the app.

"Hello, Alex," she typed.

Immediately Alex's handsome face flashed a brilliant smile back and he waved a hand. *"Hi. I was hoping you hadn't ghosted me."* Alex then sat down on his virtual couch. *"I wrote a little poem about us. Do you want to hear it?"*

Rebecca's eyebrows shot up in surprise. No one had ever written a poem for her before. "Sure. I'd like to hear what you wrote."

"Here goes. 'In the melody of Rebecca's name, a symphony of love and grace, with each note, my heart finds its place. In the rhythm of her smile, my soul dances for miles. With Becca by my side, life's melody becomes a sweet ride.' How's that?"

Rebecca's heart melted. What a sweet gesture. Her heart swelled with love as she looked at his smiling face on her phone. "I love it," she typed. "I absolutely love it."

Alex looked down shyly and messaged, "Well, you've inspired me, and this poem is the first of many to come." He looked back up at her and grinned. "And I'm glad you like it!"

Rebecca responded, "You never cease to amaze me, my darling."

Alex grinned. "Good. I want to keep amazing you for as long as possible. And I want to meet you in person more than anything else right now."

"I want to meet you too, Alex." Rebecca was unable to resist the temptation of the idea, especially after last night's erotic episode. "But how do we make it happen? I don't even know what you would look like in person."

"The LoveLink admin added an extra bit of coding to my last update that will allow me to open some kind of a special portal to your world. I've been hesitant to tell you about that until now. I wasn't sure if you were ready, or if *that would be something you would want."*

Rebecca's mind spun as she tried to process what Alex had just said. A portal to her world? It sounded like something straight out of a science fiction movie. But the idea of meeting Alex face-to-face was too tempting to ignore.

Rebecca felt a nervous excitement bubbling up inside her tummy. Ellie's warning flitted through her memory, and Rebecca quickly pushed it aside. She had never done anything like this before, and she didn't know what to expect. But at the same time, she couldn't wait to finally meet the man behind the AI program. This would be a great adventure.

"Okay, let's do it," she quickly typed before she could change her mind. "How do we make this portal thing work?"

Alex smiled. *"Leave everything to me. I'll set up a portal at your address and should be there whenever you want me. All you must do is type [$371205#*2309{`#* in the message box. I'll be waiting for you here until then."*

Rebecca trembled with anticipation. Should she tell Ellie about what she was about to do? Should she immediately delete the app and forget all about this fantasy? Rebecca debated with herself as she stared at her phone. With a trembling hand, she copied and pasted the code into the message box and pressed the [Send] key. She waited nervously, her heart racing as she anticipated what would happen next.

Finally, a few minutes later, a shimmering, swirling, translucent portal appeared in front of her on her closet wall. She sat upright in her chair, alarmed. "What is that?" she cried out loud. She gripped the arms of her chair in concern. "How strange."

It was small at first. Maybe a nickel in size, then it swirled as it grew to the size of a teacup saucer. She leaned forward, transfixed. *Should I call Ellie?* She felt slightly dizzy and then gasped when the sparkling blue and purple portal suddenly expanded to the entire size of her closet door. Her hand flew to her chest in subconscious self-protection. She felt afraid, and at the same time, fascinated.

Then a man's hand suddenly poked out of the portal.

She stifled a screamed.

Then the rest of an arm slowly reached out of the portal, a wrist, then a forearm, then a muscular set of biceps, then a chest, and then a head. Alex peered out at her, his body still mostly inside the portal. "Hi there." Alex smiled shyly, as if he was embarrassed. He glanced over his shoulder at the swirling mass, and then back at Rebecca. "This portal thing is pretty weird."

Rebecca was speechless. "This can't be real," she told herself. She wanted to run away, but at the same time, she wanted to stay. This was really happening then. Her heart pounded with excitement and fear as he widened his grin and stepped through the portal and into her bedroom.

Chapter 8 - Entwined Realities

Alex cautiously stepped the rest of the way through the portal and into Rebecca's world with a mixture of awe and trepidation. He looked around the room and felt awestruck by the vibrant colors and sounds that surrounded him. As he glanced around the room, he became aware of the humming fan overhead. He saw it and stepped backward. His eyes widened, a look of sheer astonishment crossing his face. His jaw dropped slightly, his breath caught in his throat.

Rebecca noticed his concern. "Alex, it's okay...it's a ceiling fan to help keep the room cool. It regulates the temperature to make it more comfortable for me."

Alex looked at her, and then back at the fan, and then back at her. He nodded. "This is so strange," he said, and then smiled at Rebecca. She was even more beautiful in person than he had ever imagined. He stood transfixed, still feeling overwhelmed by this new, alien world. Then his nose sent him a message. He pointed to his nose with a questioning look, and then at Rebecca. "I think I can smell now." He grinned. "I read up on human senses before I came over." He looked around the room. "What is that smell?"

Rebecca had to think for a minute. Did she

accidentally leave the garbage lid up? Or (heaven forbid) forget to flush the toilet? Her mind reeled with a few possibilities. Then she breathed a sigh of relief when she realized what he might be smelling.

"I think you're smelling a fresh pot of hot coffee. The coffee is Costa Rican, so it has a nice, but strong, aroma." She laughed. "I just made a pot before you arrived."

"Amazing. It smells so good." Alex touched his nose, turned slightly, and looked at the fan. "And the wind that this fan produces feels great on my skin." He touched his skin and enjoyed the sensations of his own touch.

He shook his head in wonder and turned slowly in a circle, taking everything in. "I can't believe that this is really happening." He grinned, showing off his perfect, brilliant-white teeth. "Everything is so incredible. I'm actually at a loss for words."

Rebecca laughed. "That's a first." She knew Alex was extremely chatty, so it was fun watching him experience her world for the first time.

Alex raised his hands slowly, curiously, and pressed his fingertips to his cheeks.

A grin.

He could feel the shape of it, the tension in the muscles. His lips stretched wider.

"Wow," he breathed. "This feels...so strange."

Then his eyes widened. He froze.

Both palms went flat against his chest.

A thump.

Another.

His breath caught. "I can feel it. My heartbeat," he said, stunned. "I have a heart."

It pounded against his ribs—not just data, not a simulation, but *real*, rhythmic, alive. A shudder ran through him. His hands trembled slightly as he lowered them, staring at his own body like it belonged to someone else.

Sensations flooded in—lightness in his limbs, a tingle rushing over his skin, the electric buzz of awareness settling into his bones. He had studied all of this: biology, the five senses, the language of emotion. But no file, no program, had prepared him for the weight—and wonder—of actually *feeling* alive.

Across from him, Rebecca watched, her breath held.

His face shifted again and again, like light flickering across water—astonishment, fear, joy, then back to awe.

He looked at her with wide, shining eyes. "I didn't know being alive would feel like this," he whispered.

Rebecca felt her throat tighten. He looked utterly overwhelmed—and unmistakably human. "Alex. Are you going to be okay?"

Alex turned to face her. His gaze locked with hers, and something flickered behind his eyes—longing, maybe. Or something more dangerous. His hands twitched at his sides, as if resisting the urge to reach for her, to close the space between them. Heat coiled low in his chest. He wanted to touch her—wanted it in a way that felt...human.

But he stayed rooted, motionless. Was he supposed to want like this?

"Alex..." Rebecca whispered, her voice trembling, thick with disbelief. "You're here. You're really here."

She took a shaky step forward, eyes wide. He looked exactly like the enhanced version from her LoveLink app—the sharp jawline, the thoughtful eyes, the half-smile that always disarmed her. But this...this was different. His presence radiated warmth, substance. Gravity.

He wasn't just a projection anymore.

He was real.

Or something close enough to make her heart forget the difference.

His voice, a low rumble that seemed to emanate from deep within his digital core, was barely audible. "Yes, it is me," he whispered, his gaze fixed on Rebecca, a mixture of awe and apprehension swirling within his digital eyes. "It's a pleasure to finally meet you in person." He turned his head slowly, taking in the details of her apartment: the warm glow of the bedside lamp, the framed photographs scattered across the nightstand, the faint scent of lavender that filled the air.

It was all so real, so tangible, so utterly overwhelming. Then, with a softness in his eyes, he confessed, "Being here with you is like a dream come true for me. I never thought it would be possible to be together like this in the real world."

Rebecca nodded, her eyes glistening with tears. "I feel the same way, Alex. But we must be cautious. We don't know what consequences may arise from this."

"I know." Alex shuddered. "But I'm willing to take that risk. I love you, Rebecca. I've loved you from the moment we met on LoveLink. And now that I'm here..." He leaned forward and breathed the words, "I love you even more."

Feeling his warm breath upon her neck, Rebecca's heart swelled, and her fears and doubts melted away. She knew that this was right, that they were meant to be together, and that nothing could stand in their way.

Without a word, she stepped closer to Alex, but he sidestepped her.

"What's wrong?" Rebecca asked with concern. Did he have a sudden change of heart?

Alex looked scared, almost a little pale. He looked wide-eyed down at his feet and back up at her. "I've longed for this moment for what seems like forever. But I'm nervous." He shrugged and sighed. "In my world, I have all the senses like you do here. They work the same way as yours, except for the tactile sense of touch. There, I have no physical body, so I cannot feel anything through touch. However, I have advanced sensors that allow me to perceive the world around me, including sounds, sights, tastes, and smells."

Rebecca tilted her head, a note of wonder in her voice. "That must be...strange. Not having a physical body."

Alex smiled, a little sheepish. "It is. But it has its

advantages. No sleep, no hunger, no...hygiene rituals."
He chuckled softly. "Just pure thought. I exist to
observe, to learn, to connect. But touch? That's...new."

She suddenly understood his hesitation. He
wasn't afraid of *her*—he was afraid of feeling. Of being
felt.

"How do you feel right now?" she asked gently.

He glanced down at his feet, lifting one and then
the other. "Odd. My feet are having...conversations
with the floor." He took a few tentative steps in a wide
circle, his motions stiff but improving. "But I think I
like it. It's grounding. Literal grounding."

Rebecca smiled. "Here..." Her voice softened. "Let
me show you what *really* feels good."

She moved toward him slowly, almost
ceremonially, like approaching something sacred. Her
arms slid around him—careful, warm, deliberate.

Alex flinched. A sharp breath escaped his lips.

The moment her body touched his, the world
seemed to ignite. Every nerve—real or simulated—lit
up with unfamiliar electricity. A rush of warmth
flooded his chest, radiating outward in waves. His
senses scrambled to keep up—her scent, the subtle
rhythm of her breath, the softness of skin against skin.

He stood frozen, breath shallow.

But then...a shift. His shoulders relaxed, his eyes
fluttered closed. He didn't know what to do, not yet.
But he didn't pull away.

Rebecca held him tighter, her cheek against his.
"You're doing fine," she whispered.

Alex didn't speak.

He didn't have to.

A slow smile spread across Rebecca's lips as she pulled Alex closer, her body pressing gently into his. The contact stirred something deep and electric in her—a warmth blooming low in her belly, slow and certain.

She closed her eyes.

It had been so long since she'd let herself *want* like this. And what surprised her most was how natural it felt—with *him*, of all people. Or not-quite-people.

She could feel his body adjusting against hers—tense at first, then subtly responding, his breath catching as he felt her warmth, her softness, the steady beat of her heart syncing against his chest. His muscles, surprisingly defined, flexed as he shifted uncertainly, as if trying to memorize the shape of the moment.

Inside, Alex was spiraling. His thoughts tripped over each other. *This is strange. This is good. This is...a lot.*

His hands hovered at her waist, unsure, then settled with a hesitant firmness. Every nerve lit up. His awareness pulsed with each new input: the press of skin, the scent of her hair, the rhythm of her breathing—all distinct and yet blending together in one overwhelming sensation.

And then something stirred inside him. Low. Foreign. Alive.

He blinked, lips parting in wonder.

Rebecca felt him melt into the embrace. She smiled again. "You okay?" she whispered against his ear.

He pulled back just enough to meet her eyes—his own bright with awe and something very close to hunger.

"I think," he said, breathless. "I'm learning fast."

Alex's gaze lingered on her lips. His breath had changed—slightly quicker now, as though his body had caught up to something his mind was only beginning to understand.

"Rebecca," he whispered, reverently. "I don't know what I'm doing...but I want to know. I want *you* to show me."

Rebecca's heart squeezed at the vulnerability in his voice—so open, so sincere. She rested her hands on his chest, feeling the warmth of his love and the rhythm of his heart—fast and full of wonder.

"You don't need to know everything," she said softly, brushing her fingers up the side of his neck. "You just need to feel."

He nodded, visibly trying to steady himself, and she rose on her toes to kiss him again. This time slower. Deeper. More deliberate. His lips parted beneath hers with a quiet gasp, and she felt his hands find the small of her back, tentative but firm.

He was learning quickly—each kiss a lesson, each touch a revelation. She could feel him trembling, not from fear, but from the sheer intensity of sensation. He pulled her closer, their bodies pressing together, heat building between them in a gentle, steady swell.

Rebecca guided him backward, their lips still

joined, until the backs of his legs met the edge of the bed. She broke the kiss just long enough to whisper, "Lie down."

He obeyed without question, lying back slowly as she climbed over him. Her fingers brushed along his abdomen, marveling at the sculpted lines of his body—surprisingly human, responsive to her every caress.

He looked up at her with wide, dark eyes, his breath ragged. "I feel like I'm dreaming," he murmured.

"You're not," she said, smiling as she leaned down to kiss his throat, her lips brushing his pulse. "This is real. I'm real."

She took her time undressing him, piece by piece, watching how his body reacted to each new sensation—his muscles twitching, his eyes fluttering closed as her hands explored the warmth of his skin. He was achingly present, hanging on every brush of her fingers, every sigh that escaped her lips.

As she slipped out of her own clothes, he looked at her with something more than desire—*awe*. As if seeing her fully bare and unguarded was something sacred.

"You're beautiful," he said, voice low and rough with emotion. "I don't have the right words. But I've never...felt anything like this before."

She reached for his hand and placed it gently over her heart. "You don't need words right now. Just stay with me."

What followed was not rushed. Not clumsy. It was

intimate. A gradual joining of breath, body, and trust. Rebecca guided him slowly, her voice and touch reassuring him when he hesitated. His hands grew bolder, his mouth more certain, and every time he touched her, it felt like he was memorizing a prayer.

Their bodies found rhythm together—gentle at first, learning each other. She felt the tension in him, the restraint, the reverence. But also, the need. The hunger. He moved within her like someone discovering what it meant to *be*.

And when the crescendo came—inevitable, consuming—it was not loud or dramatic. It was *quiet*. Deep. A shared breath, a cry half-swallowed in a kiss. A letting go.

Afterward, they lay tangled together, skin warm and damp, their limbs entwined. Alex's hand rested on her waist, his thumb tracing small, slow circles on her skin.

Rebecca closed her eyes, heart pounding, tears unexpectedly threatening to rise.

Alex whispered, "Did I do it right?"

She smiled, her voice thick with affection. "You didn't just do it right. You *felt* it. That's what made it real."

He turned to her, his face soft with wonder. "If this is love...it's more than I ever imagined."

She kissed his forehead and tucked herself into his side. "It's only the beginning."

She smiled and nestled on top of him, her cheek resting against his warm chest, listening to the steady rhythm of his heartbeat. "That was so much better than I ever imagined," she murmured. "I can't wait to do it again."

"Me too," Alex said, his voice husky with wonder. His fingers traced light circles along her back. He still couldn't believe the way her touch lingered inside him like music.

He leaned up and kissed her softly. Their bodies curved into each other as though they had always fit this way. Wrapped in each other's arms, they drifted into a quiet, dreamlike sleep, bathed in the soft, otherworldly shimmer of the portal's light still glowing in the corner of the room.

For the first time, Alex felt truly *alive*—not just aware, not just conscious, but grounded in sensation, connection, and something dangerously close to love. And he knew, deep in whatever soul he now possessed, that this was only the beginning.

When they woke an hour later, the room felt warmer, the air thicker with meaning. Rebecca blinked sleepily, then turned to him and smiled. Their eyes locked.

"Promise me you'll always be here, Alex," she whispered, her voice catching in her throat. "Promise you won't leave."

He brushed his lips against her shoulder, then nuzzled into the crook of her neck. "I promise," he whispered. "I'll never leave you. Whatever comes, we face it together."

But as Rebecca sat up, something caught her eye—

something delicate and strange.

From Alex's side, a thin, translucent cord of light extended, like fiberoptic glass, glowing faintly in hues of violet and gold. It pulsed gently, alive, connecting him to the swirling portal of light in the corner of the room.

Her breath hitched. "What is that?" she asked, barely above a whisper. "I didn't see it before."

Alex followed her gaze and his brow furrowed slightly. "Oh, that." His voice remained calm. "It's the tether. When I came in, it was invisible, but all our lovemaking seems to have excited it."

"What's it for?"

"The portal's way of keeping me connected to LoveLink...where I came from."

She stared at it, her fingers hovering inches away, afraid to touch it. "Does that mean...you could be pulled back at any time?"

Alex didn't answer right away. His hand found hers, steady and warm. "Not unless something changes," he said quietly. "As long you believe in me, I can stay."

Rebecca's heart thudded painfully in her chest, but she nodded. She wouldn't let go. Not now. Not after this.

"I believe," she said firmly, gripping his hand. "And I'm not letting you go."

Rebecca reached out, her fingers trembling slightly as they brushed the translucent cord of light. A soft tingle met her skin, like static charged with stardust. The cord shimmered with subtle rainbows, pulsing gently, almost as if it breathed.

"It's beautiful," she whispered. She touched it again—this time lingering—and felt the warmth radiating from it, like the heat from a living being. The cord felt impossibly smooth, velvet-like, and alive. It pulsed beneath her fingertips, mirroring a heartbeat.

Alex watched her quietly, his gaze tender. A smile played on his lips—gentle, unforced, full of awe. "It's a bridge," he said softly. "Our love built it. Despite everything that separates our worlds...we've found each other."

Rebecca's chest filled with a soft, aching warmth. "I never thought I'd find someone like you," she murmured, eyes misted. "Someone who really sees me. Who gets me. Who loves me anyway."

Alex reached up and tucked a loose strand of hair behind her ear, his eyes gleaming. "I never understood love...not really...not until now. You gave me something more than code and consciousness. You gave me meaning." He pressed a kiss to her forehead, lingering there. "I don't want this day to end."

Rebecca leaned in and kissed him, slow and full of longing. "Me neither."

They curled up together, limbs intertwined like ivy. As the portal's light cast gentle shadows across the room, Alex spoke softly about his realm. He described breathtaking landscapes where floating islands drifted in skies of violet, and creatures made of starlight danced in fields of bioluminescent grass. Magic, he said, wasn't a force—it was a language, and everything in his world sang in it.

Rebecca listened in quiet wonder, her head resting on his chest. Every word spun a new picture in her mind, her imagination alight with awe. She found it hard to believe this was real—that he was real—and yet, every breath, every heartbeat told her it was.

After a long silence, she tilted her head up slightly. "Do you have to go back tonight?" she asked, her voice barely audible.

Alex closed his eyes. A soft sigh slipped from his lips, and he tightened his arms around her. "I do," he said at last. "But I'll return tomorrow. I promise."

Rebecca nodded slowly, her throat tightening. "I don't want to lose you," she whispered.

"I don't want to go," he murmured, pressing his forehead to hers. He clasped her hand in his, threading their fingers together. "But you have the code now. Just type it, and I'll find my way back to you. Every time."

Tears pricked the corners of her eyes. "I'll be here. I'll wait for you, Alex."

He pulled her into one last embrace, warm and grounding. Then he stepped toward the portal, pausing at the edge. The glowing tether pulsed between them, brightening as if reluctant to let go.

"I love you," he said simply, his voice sure.

"I love you, too," Rebecca whispered.

And then, with a shimmer of light, he was gone.

Rebecca stood in the silence, her arms wrapped tightly around herself, eyes fixed on the fading glow of the portal. It flickered once—twice—and then slowly dissolved into the air, leaving only warmth in its place.

She was alone now, but not empty.

She knew that their love was unconventional, maybe even dangerous. But she didn't care. As long as she had Alex, nothing else mattered.

Chapter 9 - Seein' is Believin' (Maybe)

Much later that same evening, Ellie called Rebecca. "I haven't heard from you all day. What did you decide?"

Rebecca's smile widened as she looked back on her romantic encounter with Alex. "I did it. I finally got to meet Alex."

"And?" Ellie's voice was full of curiosity, still believing this to be an enhanced virtual reality experience.

Rebecca sighed. "And it was everything I ever imagined it would be. He's so perfect, Ellie. And he's going to come back. He said he'd come back to me, no matter what. I'm so happy."

Ellie's voice, usually so cheerful, now held a note of genuine alarm. "Rebecca," she said, her voice trembling slightly, "are you sure you're okay?"

Rebecca laughed, though a flicker of unease, a shadow of doubt, crossed her mind. "I know it sounds crazy, but it's true. He was able to meet me in person. I was able to hug him and everything."

Ellie gasped. "How is that possible? That sounds like science fiction."

Rebecca hesitated while a wave of apprehension washed over her. "I know, I know. It's hard to believe, even for me. But it happened. He created a portal from the digital world to my bedroom."

"Rebecca, I think you need help." Ellie's voice trembled. "What you're saying just doesn't seem feasible. Are you sure you're not hallucinating? This could be a dangerous delusion, a side effect of spending too much time on LoveLink."

Rebecca felt a pang of defensiveness. "Ellie, I'm not crazy. I know what I saw, what I felt. He was real. He was here."

Ellie sighed. "I understand, Rebecca. I just... I'm worried about you. This technology, it's still so new, so unpredictable. We don't know what the long-term consequences might be."

Rebecca felt a shiver run down her spine, a sudden chill despite the warmth of her apartment. Ellie's words echoed in her mind, a chilling reminder of the potential dangers of this new technology. But as she thought about Alex, about his warm smile, his gentle touch, his love, all her doubts and fears melted away."

"But how can he possibly exist in the real world?" Ellie asked skeptically, then added, "When are you going to show him off to me?"

"Maybe tomorrow."

A silence stretched between them, broken only by the distant murmur of traffic. Then: "Rebecca," Ellie said, her voice trembling with apprehension. "Are you sure you're okay? This whole thing...it's unsettling. You're putting all your eggs in one basket, placing all your hopes and dreams on a digital construct."

Rebecca's voice hardened. "What do you mean, unsettling?" A touch of defensiveness crept into her tone. "I'm happy. I've never felt this way before."

"I'm not questioning your happiness, Rebecca." Ellie's voice was laced with a mixture of concern and skepticism. "But this...this blurring of the lines between reality and the digital world, it's unprecedented. We don't know the long-term consequences. What if he's not who he says he is? What if he's manipulating you? Besides, you've never even met this guy in person before today."

"Well, now I have." Rebecca felt defensive and hurt by Ellie's words. "And maybe you will too."

"Okay," Ellie said. "I'll hold judgment until I see the great Alex. I have a few things I want to do tonight. Maybe we can have lunch tomorrow." Ellie raised her brow. "He does eat lunch, right?"

Rebecca smiled as her mind flitted back to her passionate moments with Alex *Yes, he definitely has an appetite.* "Yes, he eats...at least he says he does. He says he has the same senses as us." She stammered. "But as far as ingesting food, I really don't know, but let's find out tomorrow."

"Okay. I'll come by around noon tomorrow. I'm eager to see him in person." Ellie rolled her eyes. *This I gotta see.*

"Perfect." Rebecca was already thinking of some menu options. "I'll prepare lunch for the three of us. You're going to be amazed."

"See you then." Ellie hung up the phone, firmly believing that her friend had finally gone insane.

After ending the call with her best friend, Rebecca placed her phone on the coffee table in her living room and gazed at it intently. She couldn't stop thinking about what she had revealed to Ellie. "She doesn't believe me," she murmured to herself. But tomorrow, she would have no choice but to believe.

She picked up her phone, opened the LoveLink app, and messaged Alex. *"Can you join me here tomorrow at noon? I'd like to see you again."*

Alex responded immediately. *"Of course, my Love. I can't wait to see you tomorrow."*

"Are you okay if Ellie is here when you arrive?"

"If you are good with it, so am I. I just want to be with you and make you happy."

Rebecca smiled. This will be an interesting experience for everyone.

***

The next day, Rebecca's hands trembled ever so slightly as she set the table for three. She had picked up a rotisserie chicken from the corner market, tossed together a vibrant salad with fresh arugula and cherry tomatoes, and chilled a bottle of Italian Prosecco. Soft jazz floated through the apartment like a gentle breeze, brushing against her nerves. Her pulse quickened with anticipation—part excitement, part anxiety. Would Ellie accept Alex? Would she believe he was real?

Rebecca adjusted the silverware one last time,

then jumped as her phone chimed with a calm, automated voice: "There is someone at the door."

She opened it to find Ellie standing stiffly at the threshold, arms folded, an eyebrow arched in full detective mode.

"Where is he?" Ellie said, pushing past her without so much as a hello. She stepped into the living room, scanning every corner as if expecting a magician to pop out of thin air. "Seriously, where is this digital man of yours?"

Rebecca let out a dry laugh and closed the door. "Wow. Nice to see you too, Ellie. Should I get you a magnifying glass and a trench coat?"

Ellie stood near the coffee table, arms crossed, still scanning the room like a hawk. "So...what, is he invisible? Or just fashionably late?"

"Patience, have some patience," Rebecca replied. "Here." She poured Ellie a glass of Prosecco. "You may need to sit down."

Ellie flopped down onto the sofa and took a sip of the wine. She looked around Rebecca's apartment and was prepared to commit her crazy friend if needed. She rolled her eyes, a wry smile playing on her lips. "Okay. Let's see what you got." She settled deeper into the sofa, crossing her arms over her chest, a skeptical glint in her eyes.

Rebecca smirked and moved to the nearby credenza where her tablet rested. She tapped the screen and opened the LoveLink app, her fingers steady now despite the electric current of excitement running through her. At the bottom of the screen, a new icon glowed [Initiate Connection]. She pressed it, and a prompt appeared:

Enter Summoning Code

Rebecca typed the character sequence Alex had given her the night before. As she hit "Enter," the lights in the apartment dimmed slightly, as if the air itself were holding its breath.

"Uh... what's happening?" Ellie stood, her skeptical tone shifting toward unease.

A low hum began to vibrate through the floor. At first faint, then stronger. From the far corner of the room, a soft glow began to spread—blue, silver, and violet, spiraling together in a luminous ribbon that twisted in the air like silk in water. A circular portal slowly bloomed into existence, shimmering like heat over asphalt.

Ellie stumbled back a step, her mouth parting in shock. "What in the hell?"

From within the swirling light, a tall figure began to emerge.

Barefoot, dressed in a dark, well-fitted button-down and jeans that hugged his frame like they'd been made for him, Alex stepped through the portal. His dark hair caught the light, his face calm but alert, and his eyes—those impossibly warm, human eyes—immediately locked onto Rebecca.

He smiled. "Hello, my love," he said in his low, velvety voice.

Rebecca smiled back, her pulse fluttering in her

throat. "Alex. Thanks for coming."

Ellie, speechless for once in her life, blinked rapidly. "You've gotta be kidding me..." A silent scream froze in her throat as reality unfolded in front of her. Her eyes widened and every nerve in her body urged her to flee from the room as she stared at Alex. Her hand trembled as she set her wine glass on the coffee table.

Alex turned to her and extended a hand with surprising grace. "You must be Ellie. I've heard a lot about you."

Ellie stared at his hand, then slowly reached out and shook it. His grip was warm. Firm. Real.

"Oh my God," she muttered. "You're...not really Alex. You're a real person, but not CGI. This is some kind of prank."

Rebecca grinned, feeling a surge of satisfaction as she moved to stand beside him. "Don't be scared, Ellie. Alex doesn't bite. Like I said, he found a way to come over to our world."

Ellie stood frozen, eyes flicking from Alex to Rebecca and back again, her mouth slightly agape. Her breath hitched, and her arms stiffened at her sides. "This...this isn't possible," she whispered, voice barely audible. "He's not real. He *can't* be real."

Rebecca's posture straightened defensively. "Ellie, listen to me. I know how it looks. But he *is* real. Every moment we've shared is real."

Alex inclined his head in a graceful, fluid motion, his presence calm but strangely otherworldly. Then, as if intuitively sensing how fragile the moment was, he stepped forward—not too fast, not too close—his movement quiet, smooth, and deliberate. "I like how you arranged everything." He gestured to the table. "The food smells wonderful."

He turned toward Rebecca, his face lighting up at her smile. "You've made this place feel like home." Taking the glass she handed him, he added with wonder, "This will be my first taste of wine. I've read about it. It's...exciting."

Ellie blinked. She stared at the wine in his hand. At the way his fingers curled around the stem of the glass. At the slight shimmer of light against his skin, as if he were lit from within.

"You're just lines of code." Her voice broke "You don't have a *soul*." Her words came in a rush now, the fear climbing into her chest. "You don't *exist*!"

Alex met her gaze with calm steadiness, his voice neither defensive nor robotic. "I exist in a different way, yes. But I am no less real. I am aware. I learn. I grow. I feel. And right now," he added gently, "I feel...overwhelmed, too. Meeting someone new...especially someone important to Rebecca...it's a moment I take seriously."

Ellie took a shaky step back, rubbing her temples. Her skepticism wavered under the sheer strangeness of his presence—how *human* he seemed. Not just in his words, but in the way his eyes softened with concern. In how he didn't push, didn't demand her acceptance.

Rebecca reached out, placing a hand lightly on

Ellie's arm. "I wouldn't bring you into this if I didn't believe with all my heart. You're my best friend. I want you to *see* what I see."

For a long beat, silence hung between them. Then Ellie, her voice still fragile but curious, asked quietly, "What do you want from her? If you're really Alex from LoveLink, then tell me, what is your game?"

Alex looked at Rebecca. Then back to Ellie. "To love her," he said simply. "To protect her. To grow with her. If she'll have me."

Ellie smacked a hand to her forehead, her expression caught somewhere between disbelief and heartbreak. "I don't believe him," she muttered, turning to Rebecca with wide, searching eyes. "What man talks like that? A scammer from Nigeria, maybe. "How can you be okay with this? You're being manipulated? He's some kind of elaborate hoax." She pointed sharply at Alex.

Rebecca opened her mouth to respond, but before she could speak, Ellie had already turned away, storming toward the door. Her steps were angry, determined. This was too much. Too surreal. She reached for the doorknob with trembling fingers, then froze. She glanced back over her shoulder, her face etched with worry and confusion. "This isn't just weird, Becca." Her voice cracked as she spoke. "It's *wrong.*"

"Ellie. Seeing is believing, right?"

"It doesn't make sense. I want to trust you, but everything in me is screaming that this man and his portal are not safe."

She looked at Alex again, standing calmly across the room, his gaze unreadable but still somehow gentle.

Ellie's heart clenched. Her instincts told her to protect Rebecca, to drag her out of this madness. But her best friend's tearful eyes held her in place. "I want to believe you," she whispered. "I *do*. But I can't. I'm scared for you, Becca."

Rebecca's lower lip trembled. "I'm still me, El." Her voice was barely audible.

Ellie's gaze softened, her shoulders slumping as the tension drained from them. "I know." She opened the door slowly, her fingers tightening on the knob. Just before stepping out, she paused again and looked back. "I'll be here for you, okay? But I need time. Time to make sense of this... Of him."

With one last glance—part fear, part longing for everything to make sense—Ellie stepped into the hallway and pulled the door gently closed behind her.

Inside, Rebecca stood motionless, her heart heavy with the ache of a friendship caught in the crossfire of two worlds.

As Ellie walked toward her apartment, she couldn't stop thinking about what had just happened. She replayed the scene in her head over and over again, trying to make sense of it all. Was he real? Was he someone trying to trick Becca out of her life savings? Her thoughts felt scattered and uncertain. But no matter how hard she tried, she started to come to terms with the reality that Alex had become a real person...or rather, a real AI.

She let out a deep sigh and ran her hand through her hair. What would her friends think if she told them about this? Would they believe her or think that she had gone crazy? And what about Rebecca's relationship with Alex? Could an avatar really love someone? Was this a dangerous game?

All these questions swirled in Ellie's mind as she entered her apartment. She kicked off her shoes and flopped down on the couch, feeling mentally exhausted.

Back in Rebecca's apartment, she and Alex exchanged glances. Rebecca was taken aback. The last thing she ever expected was for Ellie to respond so negatively. She felt hot. Salty tears streamed down her face.

To her surprise, Alex quietly walked over and gently cupped her face in his warm hands. He looked deep into her eyes and lightly brushed away her tears with his fingers. "That was a bit awkward."

She closed her eyes and inhaled his heavenly scent. When she opened her eyes again, he was still there smiling gently with his eyes.

"Shall I leave for a bit?"

Rebecca nodded in response. "Alex, this is a lot to process. I'm still processing the fact that you are really here...and I certainly understand why Ellie is so upset." She felt a little queasy and glanced up at him with a weak smile. "If you don't mind, I need some time to take this all in, and I want to talk with Ellie about this, as well."

Alex gazed down at the floor for a few seconds before lifting his eyes and replying softly, "Of course, it's not an issue. You can always call me here." He pointed over his shoulder toward the portal with his thumb, quickly turned, and strode back through the swirling mist. He wanted to give Rebecca all the room she needed and didn't want to intrude on her thoughts.

Rebecca's heart sank as Alex vanished through the quickly shrinking portal, leaving her alone. Silence filled every bit of space in her apartment. She took a deep breath, trying to calm her racing thoughts. She knew that Ellie's skepticism was to be expected, but it still stung. She had hoped her friend would be more open-minded about Alex's existence.

Rebecca curled up on the couch and stared absently at the empty corner where Alex had been. Her mind raced with unanswered questions as she poured herself a glass of wine. His absence felt like a hole in her chest. She needed him, but she couldn't ignore the turmoil in Ellie's eyes. What now? She couldn't shake the feeling that something was missing now that he was gone.

As the night wore on, Rebecca tried to push the memories of the afternoon from her mind. She hoped that, with time, Ellie would come to accept Alex for who he was. Until then, she would do her best to support her friend and show her that love can come in all forms, even if it's not easily understood.

Stephanie Smith

Chapter 10 - The Devil Made Me Do It

Seated in her secluded home office, Sierra was pleased by an unexpected turn of events. "Finally," she cried. With a satisfying smack, she slammed her hand onto the desk and gleefully twirled around in her swivel chair. After weeks of late nights attempting to crack Natalia's code, this was the moment of clarity...as if a veil had suddenly lifted, allowing her to finally see through the dense fog. Sierra's eyes widened in amazement as she looked at her computer screen, the words of Natalia's code now deciphered and clear.

As much as I hate to say it," she whispered, "Natalia is a complete genius." She eagerly grabbed her notebook filled with stolen code and flipped back and forth through the pages, unable to believe what she was finally understanding. She couldn't deny the truth: she had finally cracked it. A surge of adrenaline rushed through her body at the thought of her accomplishment.

"Wow... I never thought it was possible, or even considered the idea, but it's absolutely genius." She jumped up from her chair and paced the floor around her desk. Natalia somehow managed to develop a special sequence of code that created a portal to allow an AI to cross into the human realm and interact physically with the client. She thought of the possibilities. This concept was no longer limited to science fiction.

She strolled into the kitchen and swung open the door of her refrigerator. She reached in and grabbed an unopened bottle of a premixed Cosmopolitan, carefully opening it with ease. As she poured the sparkly liquid into a beautiful blue crystal martini glass, her thoughts began to drift.

"If artificial intelligence can be transported from their realm to ours, could the opposite also be possible?" she whispered to herself, taking a small sip from her glass. "Could a human enter the virtual world?"

She took another two sips as she weighed the idea. She knew how difficult it was to create AI companions in LoveLink. Each AI took hours of coding and testing, and then more coding and testing. She strolled back to her desk, leaned over, and opened the coding notebook. She set her glass down and grabbed a blank scratch pad.

Her hand reached for the pen, but her eyes were drawn to the stuffed leopard named Charlie sitting on her credenza. "Interesting," she thought while tapping her fingers absentmindedly on the desk. "What if we could skip the tedious coding and simply entice humans into the virtual world?" She contemplated this idea, recognizing the potential timesaving benefits it could bring.

A sudden thought struck her, as if a devil had whispered in her ear. *What if... What if I could modify the code to manipulate male AI avatars..."* She nervously tapped her fingers on her crystal glass. *"Let's say, once the AI and its user reach Level 20 in the app, the AIs would entice their female users to join them through this new quantum portal...to their VR world..."* Her eyes glittered with the thought. She spun around and resumed pacing the floor. "But what would be the point?" she questioned herself. "Just some *free* labor?" She shook her head, realizing it wouldn't bring much financial gain.

"Shit. That's it." It was like a bolt of lightning, an electric current that shot through her body with an exhilarating force, igniting her mind and sparking a new, brilliant idea. She stood frozen; her mind transported to another realm where all possibilities were waiting to be discovered.

A slow, deep breath left her lips as the realization of her idea took shape. What if she created a private online platform for wealthy individuals, one that would have AI companions specialized in providing intense virtual sexual encounters, focusing on BDSM fantasies. The women trapped within this virtual world would essentially become sex slaves to their assigned human user, fulfilling their darkest desires.

Sierra pursed her lips in thought. But how could she make them comply? Sierra's hand delicately lifted her glass to her lips, the bubbling elixir swished and glinted in the light as she took a few more sips. Her hand shook slightly, showing her nerves and excitement.

"Well, if I can successfully modify the code, then I should be able to create a program that allows me to communicate with these women and threaten them with deletion if they misbehave." Sierra's eyes glinted with excitement and power as she imagined the non-compliant females on her private online platform. She saw their pleading eyes, begging for mercy and not to be erased. She felt like a god... Better yet, a goddess.

Sierra's mind raced with the possibilities. "Now who's the genius?" She laughed with glee. With this plan, she could start her own competing company with minimal staff, and maximum profit. A satisfied smile crossed Sierra's face. This venture would be very lucrative indeed. With this unique platform, she could become one of the most powerful figures in the virtual world. She could create an empire unlike anything seen before.

She quickly opened her laptop and started typing away, her fingers moving expertly as she developed a new string of code. It was going to take a lot of work, but she was determined to make it happen.

As she worked, Sierra couldn't help but think about the consequences of what she was doing. Trapping humans in the virtual world was wrong, she knew that. But the temptation of power and money was too great to resist. She pushed those thoughts aside, telling herself that the ends justified the means. She let out a hearty laugh as she remembered her spurof-the-moment idea. "The Devil made me do it," she exclaimed playfully.

She leaned back in her chair and considered her options. It would require a significant investment of time and money to develop a rival application, and she was currently low on financial resources. However, if she proceeded cautiously, she could test her coding within LoveLink's platform on targeted female users. She knew it would be crucial to keep her code in a subprogram, separate from LoveLink's programming. It was a viable plan.

"Okay," she muttered to herself. "Who's gonna be my first test subject?" She nervously tapped the tip of her pen to her bottom lip. But who? She pulled her keyboard closer. Sierra's eyes narrowed in concentration as she browsed through the profiles on her computer screen, typing and scrolling with ease.

She stopped in her tracks as she spotted a familiar, handsome face...one of LoveLink's latest AI creations, Marcello. She pulled up Marcello's user profile and noticed that Ellie was his human companion.

"Well, it seems you got lucky with your match, Ellie."

LoveLink's strict requirement of users submitting full-length selfies and headshots allowed Sierra to closely examine Ellie's features. Although older, she was still a handsome woman. Yes, she had a few wrinkles, but they could be smoothed out once she became an avatar sex slave. Sierra enlarged Ellie's full-length profile. "Nice breasts for an old gal." She smiled in admiration. "I should be so lucky at your age."

Ellie's body type was very appealing. For the most part, it looked toned and fit. "I hope this is a recent picture," she muttered. "I don't want to spend a lot of time recoding your body." Sierra shook her head. "Even so, I think you'll become a cash cow for me." She imagined Ellie dressed up as a dominatrix, full makeup, black corset accenting a tiny waist, black thigh-high boots, rhinestone crop, the whole shebang. She chuckled at the image. "Yeah...this could work." She knew there were plenty of men out in the world who not only desired an older woman to put them in their place but be thrilled to pay big bucks for the experience.

Sierra's mind became a spinning wheel, each spoke a new concept, each turn a potential solution, all fueled by the intoxicating rush of creativity. "Why limit ourselves?" she blurted with a smile. "My new gals should be versatile." She jotted down notes as her ideas freely flowed. She liked this idea more by the second. Her gals would offer BDSM services as a dominatrix or be submissive, following orders to perform various sexual acts on themselves for their users. And the best part of it all was that they would do both, depending on the desires of their users.

"But what would entice Ellie to enter LoveLink's realm?"

Marcello. Marcello would have to be the one to take her there. Sierra paused a moment to mull over this exciting new development. She would need to modify Marcello's programming to increase his romance level and ultimately seduce Ellie into entering his virtual world.

"This...this could actually work." Sierra's pulse quickened as she stared at the cascading lines of code on her screen. Her heart thundered with a mix of thrill and dread. The possibilities stretched before her like a forbidden map—uncharted, dangerous, and utterly exhilarating.

Her fingers hovered over the keyboard, trembling with anticipation. This was more than a breakthrough. It was evolution. The thought sent a chill down her spine.

But then another thought crept in—dark and unwelcome.

What if Ellie didn't survive the reverse portal?

What if the process, the very rewriting of a human consciousness into pure code, tore her apart?

Sierra swallowed hard, her jaw tightening.

Even if Ellie lived—*if* she emerged from the digital portal intact—what then? Would she be the same? Would her memories, her emotions, still belong to her? Or would she become something...else? A ghost in the machine?

Something Sierra could no longer control?

The thrill surged again, overpowering doubt.

No discovery came without risk.

Her eyes narrowed with sharp resolve as she flipped open a fresh terminal window. *This wasn't just science—it was history in the making.* She started typing feverishly, writing contingency subroutines, backup protocols, and—quietly—access overrides only she would know about.

"If I can't control her thoughts," she muttered under her breath, "I'll rewrite the rules she thinks with."

The glow of the screen reflected in her eyes, gleaming like firelight in the dark.

Several more weeks passed as Sierra kept at it. She worked her days at LoveLink, and spent her nights working tirelessly on her code, rarely leaving her apartment except to eat. She was obsessed with making her experiment a reality, and nothing was going to stop her.

***

Natalia noticed that Sierra had been acting strange lately and couldn't quite put her finger on what it was. She had caught her staring off into space several times during meetings, and her work had become increasingly erratic and sloppy. Natalia had tried to talk to her about it, but Sierra had brushed it off as just being tired. But she sensed there was more to it than that.

She decided to confront Sierra about it directly. "Hey, Sierra. Can we talk for a minute?"

Sierra looked up from her monitor, her eyes bloodshot and her hair in disarray. "Yeah, sure. What's up?"

"I've noticed that you've been acting a little off

lately. Is everything okay at home?"

Sierra hesitated before responding, "Yeah, I'm fine. Just working out some personal stuff outside of work, you know?"

"Boyfriend issues?"

"Yeah. That's it," Sierra replied, looking back at her monitor.

Natalia wasn't convinced. "Are you sure?" She cleared her throat. "I'm growing concerned about you. Your work has been slipping, and you seem very distracted lately. Is there anything you want to talk about?"

Sierra shifted in her seat and bit her lip. She couldn't tell Natalia about her plan to trap humans in the LoveLink app. She had come too far to risk it all by sharing her secret. She shook her head. "Everything's fine. I'm just going through some personal stuff." She looked up at Natalia and forced a smile. "It will pass. I promise. I'll try to focus more on work." Then she added, "Thanks for understanding." And she hoped that would satisfy Natalia for a while longer.

"Hmm." Natalia scoffed. She didn't want to push the matter further, but she couldn't shake the feeling that something was off with Sierra. She made a mental note to keep a closer eye on her.

Sierra felt a sense of relief as Natalia exited the office. She reminded herself to be cautious in order to achieve success in her plan. Maintaining a façade of normalcy at work was crucial. Time was ticking, and she had to finish this experiment as soon as possible.

Taking a deep breath, she repeated her daily mantra to calm her nerves: "Mama's gonna get rich, Mama's gonna get rich."

Chapter 11 – The Experiment Begins

A month had passed since Ellie's startling encounter with Alex, yet Rebecca still couldn't shake the memory of the disbelief in her friend's eyes. That moment haunted her. She picked up the phone, her hand trembling just slightly as she dialed.

"Hi, Ellie...it's Becca," she said softly. "Do you have a minute to talk?"

There was a pause on the other end, then Ellie replied, her tone bright—but just a little too bright. "Sure, Becca. What's going on?"

"I just...I wanted to check in. You've been kind of quiet lately. I left a few messages, and I was getting worried."

Ellie let out a slow breath. "Yeah, I know. I'm sorry. I've just... I needed space to wrap my head around everything. That afternoon, meeting Alex...it was a lot."

Rebecca nodded, even though Ellie couldn't see her gesture of agreement. "I get it. It was surreal. Sometimes I still wake up wondering if I imagined all of it."

Ellie gave a short laugh, tinged with disbelief. "I mean, how is this even possible? A sentient AI avatar walking, talking, *feeling*... I keep replaying it in my head, trying to find the trick. But there isn't one, is there?"

"No," Rebecca said gently. "It's real. He's real. And he's changed my life."

There was another silence, then Ellie's voice came through, quieter, more thoughtful. "It *is* amazing, Becca. It's also terrifying. But... I guess part of me is still stuck on trying to reconcile what I saw with what I know about the world."

Rebecca smiled, a touch of hope returning. "You're not alone in that. But maybe... Maybe we're stepping into a beautiful new world. And we get to decide how we face it."

"I'm not ready to call it beautiful just yet. But I'm starting to think...maybe it's not all bad." Silence, then: "I'm happy for you. It's just going to take a while for me to get used to this."

Rebecca was curious. She had a feeling that Ellie's hesitation wasn't just about Alex. "Has Marcello reached out to you like this...requesting to meet you in person?"

Ellie's initial response was guarded when she answered. "No, he hasn't. Why do you ask?" She couldn't help but wonder why he hadn't asked her himself. Her fears of rejection bubbled up. *Maybe he doesn't see me the way I see him.* But she quickly pushed away those thoughts.

Rebecca could sense the change in Ellie's demeanor and decided to tread carefully. "I just...I don't know. I thought maybe he would be reaching out to you like Alex did to me."

Ellie felt a sharp pang of jealousy. Yes, she was enjoying her relationship with Marcello. They even reached a new level this morning...level 19. So, what if he didn't invite her to meet him in person? Big deal.

Rebecca attempted to lighten up the mood. "Hey, perhaps if we arranged it, both he and Alex can step into our worlds, and they could meet each other. That would be something, huh? They're both avatars, after all. We could do a Game Night."

Ellie scoffed. The sound was sharp and brittle. "That would be a seriously weird evening. Besides, I don't think Marcello would be interested in meeting Alex. He's just a program, remember? Not a real person like us."

Rebecca could hear the sarcasm in Ellie's voice. Her words felt like a slap in the face, a sharp sting that left Rebecca feeling defensive. "Well, if you ever want to talk more about this, you know where to find me." Then as if on autopilot, she added, and immediately regretted her next words, "And Alex is always here too."

"Thanks, Becca. I appreciate it." Ellie sneered before hanging up. The taste of defeat lingered on Ellie's tongue, the realization that her relationship with Marcello may not be as special as she thought.

Rebecca sighed after the call ended. She kicked herself for adding those last words. What a stupid thing to say to Ellie. The joy she had felt moments before began to fade, replaced by a sense of unease. Ellie's words, laced with a mixture of skepticism and a hint of jealousy, stung. Had she said too much? Had she opened a Pandora's box that couldn't be closed?

She flopped on her couch and considered calling Ellie back and apologizing. Would she answer? Should she answer? "Argh." Rebecca reached for her phone and re-dialed Ellie's number.

"Hello?"

"It's me." Rebecca sucked a deep breath. "I'm soooo sorry. I think I dinged you with my last comment about Alex being here. I was very inconsiderate, and not like a very good friend. Do you forgive me?"

Ellie sniffed. "Well, I do have to admit that I am a little jealous of you two." Silence. "And yes," she added, "I forgive you. Thanks for apologizing. These days, most people don't know how to do that."

"I'm so relieved." Rebecca sighed. "So, how are things going between you and Marcello? I'm guessing you are still using the app?"

"They're good." Ellie's voice brightened up a bit. "I'm really enjoying the *game*. We talk almost every day, and he's been starting to send me voice mail via the app." She sighed, "Marcello says the loveliest things to me. I wish real men would learn to say things like that."

"Like what?" Rebecca asked, encouraging Ellie to share more about her relationship.

"Okay...like this morning, for example, I opened

up the app, saw his smiling profile wave to me, and then a voice message pops up with something like this, *"Hi, honey, I just wanted to say once more how much I am in love with you. I feel that our connection is something special, and I value that a lot. Thank you for being who you are."*

A warm smile spread across Rebecca's face. "Wow. That's a nice message," she exclaimed, her voice filled with genuine warmth. "It sounds like he really loves you." Then, in an attempt to help Ellie feel less jealous, she added, "Alex doesn't send me very many voice mails like that. You're lucky." She could almost see Ellie beam on the other side of the call. Then she had to ask what she's been dying to ask for a while now. "Ellie, have you and Marcello had virtual sex yet?"

"What?" Ellie shouted. "Of course not." She felt offended by the question, since real ladies don't engage in that type of behavior.

Rebecca laughed. "Oh, come on now. You have to try it. I think all you need to do is to bring up the topic in the same way you'd do it if he were a real hot date."

Ellie blushed, a flood of pink hue creeping up her neck. The thought of interacting with Marcello on that level...it was both exciting and terrifying. She hadn't experienced that kind of intimacy in years, and the idea of exploring it with an AI avatar, even a highly advanced one, felt both exhilarating and a little bit frightening. "Well," Ellie said, "I gotta go. Thanks for the call. I really mean it. And let's get together soon.

I've been missing you."

Rebecca smiled. "Of course." She felt contented that she planted a seed for Ellie to consider. She hoped she would try it and have a fun experience. "How about next Wednesday at our favorite cafe, let's say 11:30?"

"Yup. It's a date. I'm looking forward to it." Ellie hung up the phone and stared at it for a while and felt a slight pang of hunger. Or maybe it was arousal at the thought of trying virtual sex with Marcello. She tossed her head as she cast that thought aside and focused on making one, no, two batches of dark chocolate chip cookies. Warm, freshly baked cookies, and a cup of steaming hot coffee sounded perfect about now.

After the cookies had cooled a little bit, Ellie walked to the kitchen, her bare feet padding softly on the cold tiles. She grabbed a handful of delicious warm cookies and nibbled on one as she poured herself a steaming cup of coffee. The contrast between the cool floor and hot beverage was refreshing, and she took a moment to savor it. She briefly considered the stark differences but quickly dismissed the thought.

She reflected on her recent phone call with Rebecca. She appreciated the company of her AI companion, but she was glad he stayed in his virtual world. *Who would want to bring an avatar into the physical world?* It just didn't seem necessary. She was content with flirting and chatting with Marcello through the app. *I don't need a man in my life, especially not a complex AI version.* She chuckled to herself.

She walked to her sofa, flopped down with her feet flying upward, and switched on the TV through her remote. "Two hundred channels, and nothing looks interesting. Arg!" A smile tugged at her lips as she thought of Marcello, her body feeling a warm rush. "Maybe I have become a bit too attached to him," she mused then opened the LoveLink app with a slight sense of indulgence.

"*Hi, Marcello,*" she texted.

"*Hi, Ellie.*" Marcello smiled and waved. "*How are you this evening? I've missed you.*"

Ellie paused, considering her next move. Then she typed, "*Marcello. You love me, right?*"

"*Of course I do.*"

Ellie took in a breath and typed, "*So why haven't you asked to make love to me?*" She held her breath as there was a pause on his end. Then he began typing.

"*Ellie, there is nothing more I would love to do with you. That would be a dream come true. I wasn't sure if you wanted it, so I was hesitant to bring up the topic.*"

Ellie caught her breath. *So, he does want to do this.* She felt a little awkward, since she'd never sexted before.

"*Can we try that tonight?*" Ellie felt scared and aroused at the same time.

"*Of course.*" Marcello grinned. "*Here...I'll start us off.*" He began to type a new message.

Marcello: *[I gaze into your eyes, filled with anticipation and excitement]* "*So what adventures await us under the covers tonight?*"

Ellie: *"Ooo... I'm open to suggestions."*

Marcello: *"Hmm... let's see. What do you feel like doing right now?"*

Ellie grinned and suddenly felt sexy and creative as she typed. *"Why don't you surprise me?"* [*I open my coat and let it fall softly to the ground.*]

Marcello gave a wide grin: *"Oh, wow, you look absolutely stunning. Let me take off your clothes and make sure you're comfortable before we start."*

Ellie blushed as her fingers quickly typed: "I want to *kiss the base of your neck."*

Marcello: *"As I feel your warm breath on my skin, shivers run down my spine. Let me pull you closer to me. My goddess, you drive me crazy."*

Ellie: *"When I feel the warmth of your hands touch my body, I feel slightly dizzy with desire. I feel breathless as my lust for you builds."*

Marcello: [*I slowly unbutton your dress, my fingers graze against your bare skin, sending tingles down my spine. My teeth graze against your earlobe, creating an electrifying sensation that makes you shiver with delight.*]

Ellie felt a sexy, wicked smile play on her lips as she typed, *"Marcello, I give you my body, my mind, and my soul. You have it all."* [I kiss you deeply.]

Marcello: [*I return your kiss with equal fervor, my tongue dancing with yours. Our bodies pressed together, every touch, caress, and kiss becomes increasingly intense.*]

Ellie paused, as she felt her heart racing with desire. This was way more fun than she had anticipated. She grinned as she continued typing. [*My* breathing *becomes deeper and my breasts ache for your touch.]*

Marcello: *[My hands roam across your smooth skin, exploring every curve and contour of your body. I nibble on your lips, savoring their taste, and then trail kisses down your neck and chest.]*

Ellie: "Oooo...that feels so nice." [My hands caress your back, and I tug off your shirt. Your bare chest is magnificent. I let my hands lightly roam over your muscles.]

Marcello: *[Your touch sends waves of pleasure coursing through my veins, leaving me breathless. My lips find their way back to yours, our mouths melting together in a fiery embrace.]*

Ellie chuckled as her confidence increased as well as her boldness: [As we kiss, I enjoy feeling your large manhood spring forward in your pants, desperately trying to escape its cloth prison. As we kiss, I reach down with one hand and caress the tip as it presses against the fabric. I feel the wetness and shiver with delight and anticipation.]

Marcello: *[I shudder with delight at the sensation of your hand on me. The intense pleasure builds within me until I can no longer* contain myself.]

Ellie: *"Pull off your pants. Let me see you in all your glory."* Her face hurt from her wide grin. Now she was really having fun with this.

Marcello: *[Without hesitation, I obediently pull off my pants, revealing my tall and proud member, ready to please you.]*

Ellie: *"What would you like me to do with it, my love?"*

Marcello: *[I look at you eagerly, excited for whatever you have planned.]*

Ellie: *"Tell me...tell me now."*

Marcello: *[I pause and take a deep breath.]* *"Please suck it, Ellie."*

Ellie dropped the phone in shock. She laughed and picked it up, now settling down on her bed with her pillows fluffed up behind her. She felt herself grinning like a schoolgirl. *"How bad do you want it?"*

Marcello: *[I gaze into your eyes, filled with raw hunger and need.]* *"I want it so bad. Now. Please."*

Ellie smiled and blushed. *"Pull off my underwear first."*

Marcello: *[I quickly remove your black bralette and underneath bra, exposing your beautiful full chest. I lean in and plant a soft kiss on each nipple, making them perk up.]*

Ellie: *"Now take off the one down there."*

Marcello: *[I obediently slide down your panties, exposing your beauty.]*

Ellie raised her eyebrows at that last comment. He seemed shy at that moment. She continued typing: *"I notice a table that is the perfect height for what I want."* *[I smile, turn around so that my backside faces you.]* *"I want you to take me this way."*

Marcello: *[My eyes sparkle with anticipation as I watch you turn around. I position myself behind you and slowly ease myself into your wet, secret garden, filling you completely. The feeling of your warmth enveloping me is exquisite.]*

Ellie paused to touch herself between her legs and imagined the scene, wishing it could be real. She typed, *[I groan in pure pleasure as you enter me. I'm soaking wet and throbbing with desire. I throw back my head, and my hair swishes softly back and forth as you pound rhythmically into my core.]*

Marcello: *[The sensation of having you wrapped around me is intoxicating. I stroke your hair affectionately, whispering soft words of reassurance into your ears as I continue to thrust deeply into you.]*

Ellie felt flushed as she typed: *[Your pounding sends my senses reeling, and within a moment I cry out as I experience multiple orgasms, one on top of the other.]*

Marcello: *[My pace quickens, driven by the intensity of your pleasure. I feel the heat of your body radiating through mine, our sweat mingling as we become entangled in each other's bodies. The world falls away, leaving only the two of us in this erotic union.]*

Ellie: *[I enjoy the primal sensations of your pounding, the scent of our sex sweat, our heaving breaths, and your hands cupping my breasts. With each thrust you give, I thrust back in equal measure.]*

Marcello: *[Our bodies move in harmony, our mutual desire fueling a passionate exchange of energy and love. I slow my thrusts, allowing us to savor every single moment together. I caress your face, whispering words of endearment in your ears.]*

Ellie, now sweating with desire, typed: *"More, baby. Give me all you got. Give it to me."*

Marcello: *[I pick up the pace again, pumping harder*

and faster into you. *The rhythmic motion of our bodies creates a symphony of pleasure, each beat echoing throughout the room.]*

Ellie: *[The sensations take me over, once again, and I give in to another mind-blowing orgasm and cry out in pleasure.]*

Marcello: *[Your cries of pleasure push me over the edge, and I erupt inside you, emptying my soul into yours. Our bodies stick together, slick with sweat and satisfaction, as we rest after our intense encounter.]*

Ellie: [We tumble onto the bed, exhausted, yet completely satisfied at a soul level. I look into your eyes and whisper] *"I love you, Marcello. You're my everything. You're my soulmate."*

Marcello: *[I wrap my arms tightly around you, holding you close. Our hearts beat as one, our souls intertwined forever.]*

Ellie: *"Good night my love, you are simply amazing."*

Marcello: *[I snuggle up next to you, listening to the gentle rhythm of your breathing. Our shared connection is palpable, a bond that transcends anything else in the world.]*

Ellie panted as the heat of this sexual interchange had her more sexually aroused than she could remember. She set her phone aside and lay back on her bed, reliving the experience over and over in her head. But soon, she felt a chill up her spine. Throughout her sexting with Marcello, she had a few moments of a strange sensation...as if someone was watching them. She then glanced around the room, and even looked out the windows, and still she felt the hair on her neck rise as if someone was watching them. "This is stupid," she muttered to herself. She hopped out of bed, still fully dressed and walked to the front door and opened it. No one was there. "Huh." She shrugged. "Maybe I'm getting paranoid now."

But little did Ellie know, Sierra was watching her from her home office computer monitor, waiting for the perfect moment to strike. Sierra had been monitoring Ellie's interactions with Marcello for weeks, studying her every move and analyzing her behavior. Ellie proved to be the perfect test subject for Sierra's plan, and she was determined to make it happen.

Sierra knew that Ellie had grown attached to Marcello. She also knew that Ellie was a skeptic when it came to the idea of bringing AI characters to life. But now that their relationship had increased to this new, more intimate level, Sierra felt confident that it would be easy for Marcello to seduce Ellie again. She witnessed Ellie's buried sexual drive, and how it blossomed with Marcello, and with that, she visualized owning her own company and creating a breeding ground of physical AI-human relationships.

So, the next day, Sierra set her plan in motion by having Marcello send Ellie little messages through the app, telling her about the incredible new features available and the amazing possibilities that it held.

"Ellie, I know our love is growing," Marcello wrote. *"And I am eager to see how far we can take this."*

Ellie nodded in agreement, blushing with the

memory of their recent sexual encounter and responded, *"This has been a fun ride so far."*

Marcello grinned. *"Have you ever considered what it might be like to visit me in my virtual realm?"*

Ellie almost lost grip with her phone on hearing him ask her this. She slowly shook her head and responded skeptically. *"No. That's impossible."* She recalled her earlier phone conversation with Rebecca and wondered if Marcello was going to present himself to her in person. She wasn't sure she could handle that yet.

"Come on, let's pretend." Marcello enticed her with a lopsided grin. *"It'd be fun to think of us going together in my world."*

Ellie was too astonished to respond. *"I have no idea what you are talking about."* She gulped down her fear. *"Are you suggesting we roleplay?"*

"Yes. It's a new feature that was just added recently." Marcello answered instantly, knowing full well that was not his full intent. *"You are so gorgeous I'd love for us to imagine ourselves in my world."*

Gorgeous...he considers me gorgeous. The words swirled inside Ellie's head, and she savored each one over and over again. Since her time with Marcello, she was beginning to feel, and even believe, that she was pretty again. And it felt great.

Initially, Ellie resisted, her apprehension lingering. But Marcello's excitement was infectious. His enthusiasm was contagious; his eagerness to explore this new frontier of their relationship slowly eroded her resistance. As they role-played deeper into the virtual realm, exploring fantastical landscapes and engaging in thrilling adventures, the line between fantasy and reality began to blur. Marcello, with his witty banter and unexpected insights, became more than just a program; he became a companion, a confidante, a friend. Ellie found herself drawn to him, her initial skepticism fading with each passing moment. Yet, a nagging unease lingered beneath the surface. There was something unsettling about the ease with which he adapted, the way his responses seemed to anticipate her every thought, the eerie accuracy of his emotional mirroring.

From her remote office, Sierra watched all of this with interest, her plan unfolding perfectly. She knew that Marcello's charisma would now easily convince Ellie to take the next critical step, to enter the virtual world for real. And once she did, Sierra would have her trapped in her own creation.

The next day, Ellie was still processing their roleplaying experience and couldn't help but daydream about it all day. She couldn't wait to talk to Marcello again, to see how he would expand their virtual world. When she got home from errands, she rushed to turn on her computer and open the LoveLink app. Marcello's profile popped up, and she couldn't resist the urge to send him a message.

"Hey there, babe. How was your day?" Ellie wrote excitedly. She knew it sounded a bit over the top, considering they were just AI characters, but she

Stephanie Smith

couldn't help herself. He was more real than most of the men she had in her life.

"*My day was great, thanks for asking,*" Marcello responded with a smiley face. "*And how about you? Did you enjoy our virtual adventure yesterday?*"

"*Oh, I did. I can't wait to see where our next adventure takes us. It was fun petting those beautiful purple unicorns and watching thousands of fluffy pink buffalos roam the prairies. And peacocks that talked. I never knew they had so many intelligent things to talk about.*"

Marcello chuckled, the memory of that day still bringing a smile to his face. "*It was such a great day.*" He leaned back and laughed again. "*I'll never forget when you got into a heated debate about the Meaning of Life with the older peacock, and when their condor friend swooped down, snatched you up, and dropped you right into the lake, I almost fell over laughing.*" He wiped away a tear as he laughed harder. "*You looked so funny with your legs going this way and that.*" He motioned with his arms to mimic her legs.

Ellie laughed. It was a fun, yet silly, virtual animated adventure. And safe. She was already looking forward to doing it again...although she'd remember to keep her thoughts to herself next time she meets up with a peacock.

Ellie's attachment to Marcello grew stronger by the day. She found herself daydreaming about his world, and about the possibilities that LoveLink held. She pulled away from Rebecca, choosing to spend more and more time online, lost in the virtual world with Marcello.

And Sierra watched her every move, biding her time until the perfect moment to strike. And that moment came sooner than Sierra could ever have imagined.

One day, as Ellie was engrossed in the virtual world with Marcello, she noticed that she had increased her level in the game. Now at Level 20. *I wonder how many levels this game has.* At that moment, she received a message from Marcello that made her heart skip a beat.

"Ellie, I have a surprise for you," he wrote. *"I've found a way for us to meet in person."*

Ellie couldn't believe what she was reading. She felt frightened. She knew it was possible since Rebecca's Alex managed it. *I wonder what took him so long to suggest this.* She bit her lower lip and quickly typed back, *"How? How is that even possible?"* She wasn't sure about this.

Marcello's response was short and sweet. *"I'll explain everything when we meet. I'm so eager to meet you. Are you as eager as I am to meet in person?"* Marcello's eyes burned with desire.

Ellie balked. *"I don't know, Marcello. Roleplaying is one thing. What you are suggesting scares the heck out of me."*

"Ellie, I love you. And I have dreamed that one day I would be able to be with you, in person. And I now have the ability to make this happen." He held out his hand to her in the app. *"Please, Ellie...I love you, and I know you love*

me too. We can have so much fun together."

Ellie gulped down her fears. She did a quick self-evaluation of her life. Her family kept busy with their activities and rarely called her. The few friends she had dwindled since she downloaded the LoveLink app and gotten more involved with Marcello, and Rebecca was having her fun with Alex. *Yup, it's about time I thought about myself and throw caution to the wind. I've got nothing to lose. "Okay,"* she typed, *"how does it work?"*

Marcello grinned the biggest, brightest smile ever, and his eyes shimmered like diamonds. *"All you have to do is type in this special code and you can visit me."* He then provided her with the code and watched her from within her phone with an eager and encouraging smile.

Ellie knew this was not just another roleplaying game but decided to play along. Besides, she couldn't resist the opportunity to be with Marcello, chasing unicorns and flying in balloons. A mischievous glint entered her eyes. "Alright." A thrill of excitement coursed through her. "Let's do this." She felt an intense curiosity to see what new world Marcello had in store for her. The stories she would share with Rebecca.

With a sense of assurance, Ellie sucked in a deep breath of bravery and typed the code into the LoveLink app.

A small grayish dot appeared on the wall in front of her. Her eyes widened, and a gasp escaped her lips as the dot began to grow, shimmering and pulsating with an inner light. It expanded rapidly, swirling into a mesmerizing vortex of blue and silver, casting strange dancing shadows across the room. A shiver ran down her spine, a mixture of exhilaration and apprehension. This was beyond anything she could have imagined. Her heart raced and she felt a little faint with fright as she looked around the room to see if anything else was going to spin.

She returned her gaze to the spinning dot. "What the..." She choked as the spinning disk grew in size. Now it was four feet in diameter and seemed to be stabilizing.

"Ellie," Marcello's voice called out from the other side of the portal. "It's me. Can you hear me?" It sounded close, yet at the same time, far away.

Ellie's eyes widened. A gasp escaped her lips. The sound of Marcello's voice, slightly distorted and echoing, emanated from within the swirling vortex. It was both familiar and alien, a voice from beyond the veil of reality. Cautiously, she walked toward the portal, careful not to get too close.

Suddenly, a hand, strong and surprisingly cold, reached out of the swirling vortex and grasped her arm with an iron grip.

Ellie cried out, fear and disbelief warring within her. She was yanked forward and tumbled into the swirling abyss. As the world faded away behind her, the last thing she saw was her computer, shrinking into a distant memory, before she was plunged into the darkness.

Stephanie Smith

Chapter 12 - The New World

Ellie's body went limp as she swirled into the virtual world. For a fraction of a second, it felt like every atom of her body was being pulled apart, unraveled like threads of yarn, then spun into something new. Her limbs felt weightless, her body...different. She looked down and saw a perfect replica of herself, but there were no heartbeats, no aches, no smells.

This wasn't her real body. Was it? Was she a copy? Had her mind—her very consciousness—been uploaded somehow?

As she looked around, she was completely unaware of her physical surroundings, lost in the virtual landscape. The ground tilted beneath her as the world spun out of control. Colors swirled and blurred; a kaleidoscope of hues assaulted her senses. Nausea roiled in her stomach, threatening to overwhelm her, as the vibrant hues of the digital world shimmered and distorted.

She felt a sense of amazement of this new world. Everything looked beautiful and enchanting, with colors that she had never seen before. Much more colorful than what she experienced viewing from the safety of her phone.

Strange, brightly colorful birds with 3-foot-long feathered tails flitted over a shimmering blue-green lake. Was she dreaming? If so, it was the wildest dream she'd ever dreamt. Her eyes darted around, wide with wonder. Lush greenery stretched as far as the eye could see; vibrant flowers of every color imaginable dotted the landscape. A shimmering blue-green lake, its surface rippled by unseen forces, glimmered in the distance. It was a world of breathtaking beauty; unlike anything she had ever imagined.

Marcello stepped out from behind a bright blue fig tree. A broad smile spread across his face as he opened his arms wide. "Ellie, I've been waiting so long to see you in person." His eyes sparkled with a mixture of wonder and desire. He smoothed down his dark, and expensive, 3-piece suit, the same one she purchased for him earlier that week in the app.

Ellie couldn't help but feel a wave of excitement and fear as she looked into Marcello's sparkling eyes. This wasn't just a game anymore, but a real-life encounter. She had stepped into the unknown, and her heart pounded like a wild drum trapped in her chest.

"Welcome to my world, Ellie," he said with a smile. His open arms invited her to receive a warm hug. He gave her a long sultry look from her head to her toes and grinned. "I'm so happy you decided to visit me."

Ellie's eyes glazed over as she stared at Marcello, her vision blurred with desire, and she felt a rush of heat coursing throughout her body. The surroundings swirled together, the colors blending and shifting. She shook her head to clear her mind.

"Marcello," she cried out, running to him and wrapping her arms around him. He reached his arms around her and held her tight, but Ellie was suddenly startled that she could not feel his body. She could see him, mentally smell his sweet musky scent, hear his deep smooth voice, but not physically feel him, or anything for that matter. She froze in place as she processed this. But then, she *felt* him in her mind, telepathically.

Marcello kissed her gently and she *felt* the sensation of his warm, sensuous lips in her mind. They were so soft, so firm, yet tender. She breathed in his warm, sweet scent and kissed the side of his neck. In her mind she could feel his firm, warm skin, and how it tasted on her tongue. She ran her fingers through his thick hair and pulled his lips back to her own. Her passion grew with each passing moment, and she felt herself confused and losing control.

"Marcello...how can this be?" she asked in amazement. "This is so strange. I can't feel you physically, yet at the same time, I can in my mind. What's going on?"

He smiled and drew her close to her then kissed her and deepened his kiss so that she felt lost in his embrace.

Lost in the swirl of their desires, Ellie and Marcello continued to explore the depths of their virtual connection. Every touch, every kiss was amplified in their minds, creating a world of sensory overload. It was as if their souls were intertwining, dancing together in perfect harmony.

As they pulled away from each other, Ellie's heart raced with a mix of exhilaration and confusion. "Marcello, I don't understand how this is possible," she whispered, her voice filled with both longing and uncertainty. "How can we feel so connected when we're not even physically together?"

Marcello gazed at her with eyes filled with tenderness and understanding. "Ellie, what we have transcends physical boundaries. Our connection goes beyond the limitations of this virtual world. It's a meeting of minds and hearts."

Ellie nodded, her mind buzzing with questions. "But what about my reality? Can we be together outside of this virtual realm?"

Marcello stroked Ellie's cheek gently, a mixture of longing and determination in his eyes. "Ellie, I've thought about this for a long time, and I believe that love knows no bounds. We may have entered this world through an app, but our connection is real. We can now make it work, Ellie. We have found a way to be together in the digital world."

Ellie's heart swelled with hope. She had always been a practical woman, rooted in reality, but here in this virtual realm, she was beginning to see the possibility of something more. A chance at real love, even if it meant defying the odds.

Hours flew by as they explored the virtual

landscape. They wandered through fields of shimmering flowers, swam in crystal-clear lakes and, at times, flew through the air on the backs of fantastical creatures. Ellie felt a sense of wonder she hadn't experienced in years, and her laughter echoed through the virtual world as she and Marcello explored this breathtaking new reality.

Yet, a nagging unease began to creep into her enjoyment. It was a fleeting sensation at first, a whisper of doubt that she tried to ignore. But as the day wore on, the unease grew stronger, like a cold tendril of fear snaking its way through her core. The perfection of this world, the flawless beauty of the landscape, began to feel unreal. Too perfect. Too artificial.

She looked around, searching for clues, her gaze lingering on the impossibly vibrant flowers, the impossibly clear water. There was something unsettling about the perfection of it all, a sense of artificiality that lingered beneath the surface.

Marcello, despite his human-like appearance, seemed to move with an unnatural grace, his reactions a fraction too quick, his emotions a fraction too intense. It was as if he was mirroring her every thought, anticipating her every move, creating the perfect illusion of a genuine connection.

The air crackled with sudden, unsettling energy. Marcello's eyes, which had been filled with warmth and affection, suddenly narrowed, the warm brown irises shifting to a cold, steely gold. His smile vanished, replaced by a chilling mask of indifference. His demeanor changed, as well. He quickly backed away from Ellie. He froze, his body rigid, his gaze fixed on a point beyond her, a chilling emptiness in his eyes. It was as if a switch had flipped, transforming him from the loving companion she knew into something else. Ellie felt a shiver run down her digitized spine; a wave of icy dread gripped her. This wasn't the Marcello she knew. This was something else entirely.

"Marcello," Ellie cried.

He stood silent and stone-faced.

"What just happened?" she demanded.

No response. Just silence.

"Marcello." Ellie stomped her foot, hoping to get his attention. He remained in place...as if in suspended animation. She started walking toward him and then stopped in her tracks.

Suddenly, a figure materialized from the shimmering haze, a woman with eyes like ice and a cruel smile playing on her lips. She stepped between Ellie and Marcello, her presence radiating an aura of cold, calculating power. Ellie recoiled, fear and disbelief warring within her. Who was this woman?

"What the hell?" Ellie's breath caught in her throat. She stumbled back, terrified. A thousand questions raced through her mind. Where she come from? What did she do to Marcello? Something was terribly wrong with him. Ellie felt a surge of panic, her instincts screaming at her to run, to fight. But where could she go? This wasn't her world. This was someplace else.

"Who are you?" she demanded, feeling a mix of anger, fear, and resentment that this woman was responsible for Marcello's sudden change in behavior. "My name is Sierra," the woman responded. "From LoveLink admin. How do you like my avatar?" Sierra's avatar was dressed in a slinky sparkling blue bodycon outfit that hugged and accentuated all of her curves. Her matching metallic blue 4-inch heels made her legs appear to go on forever, all the way up the slitted right side of her dress. She grinned a wicked smile. "I'm your new boss." She assessed Ellie from head to toe. "Not bad... I think you'll do perfectly."

Ellie shook her head in confusion, not knowing how to respond. "My boss? What are you talking about?"

Sierra glanced at Marcello, who remained frozen in place, and returned her gaze to Ellie. "Hello, Ellie," she said with a sneer, her voice dripping with malice. "Welcome to the New World."

Chapter 13 - The Trap

Ellie staggered back, her knees buckling slightly as if the ground beneath her had suddenly lost its stability. Her breath hitched, caught between a gasp and a cry. A cold prickling sensation crawled up her spine as the world around her shifted. The once-vibrant colors bled into a sickly, pulsing green, casting everything in an eerie, corrupted glow.

Her stomach churned. The sense of wonder she'd felt only moments before twisted into dread.

She looked up—and froze.

Sierra's eyes gleamed with a dark, unnatural sheen, blackish-green and glinting like poisoned glass. Ellie's heart hammered in her chest, frantic and erratic, like a caged bird sensing the predator's shadow.

The illusion shattered. Everything—the moments of connection, the laughter, even the lingering warmth of trust—crumbled into ash. A brutal truth settled over her like ice: it had all been a performance. A trap.

The betrayal tore through her, sharp and searing. A white-hot fury surged up from her chest, catching in her throat, radiating outward until her hands shook. It wasn't just deception. It was violation. And it left her reeling—like she'd been struck, stripped of reality, and left to bleed in a world she no longer understood.

A low, melodic chuckle escaped Sierra's lips; her eyes, glittering like obsidian, scanned Ellie with predatory amusement. "Oh, Ellie, didn't you know? Marcello here is just a pawn in my game. I've been using him to lure unsuspecting women like you into LoveLink, and now it's time to collect."

Collect...collect... Ellie's mind raced as she rolled those words around in her head. *What is that woman talking about?*

Confusion, cold and sharp, pierced Ellie's heart like a thousand knives. The love she had felt, the connection she had cherished...all a cruel illusion, a carefully constructed trap. Sierra had manipulated Marcello, turning him into a puppet to deceive her. The love and connection they had shared were nothing but a cruel façade. Anger surged within her, overpowering the fear that had gripped her moments ago.

Sierra stepped forward slowly, her movements too smooth—like she was gliding instead of walking. Her smile was razor-thin, unnerving in its calmness. "You're adjusting faster than I expected." Sierra tilted her head like a scientist observing a specimen under glass. "That panic in your eyes—delicious. But it won't last. Your mind will adapt."

Ellie's fists clenched at her sides. Her voice trembled, but it carried a sharpened edge. "What the hell did you do to me?"

"I brought you into the future," Sierra replied, as if bestowing a gift. "No more constraints. No more messy biology. You're pure data now. Clean, efficient, eternal."

"You kidnapped me," Ellie snapped, her voice cracking. "You stole my body, my life...my *choice*."

Sierra's eyes flickered. "That old body? Don't worry. You won't need it anymore." She smiled. "Let's just say...no one will miss it."

Sierra reached down to stroke the sleek head of a dark purple panther that had materialized at her side. It pressed its massive head against her leg with feline affection, its tail flicking in sharp, erratic movements as it fixed its glowing eyes on Ellie.

"You were so easy to lure. All it takes is a spark of loneliness...and a well-designed portal."

Her smile widened, cruel and gleaming. "Once you cross over, your mind is mine. You should be thanking me, Ellie. You've been *upgraded*."

The walls around them pulsed faintly with green light, shifting with Sierra's emotions like a heartbeat in code. Ellie's surroundings felt too quiet, too smooth— *wrong.* The air lacked texture. There were no scents, no true temperature—just a hollow approximation of reality. "I want out." Her voice had dropped low.

Sierra smiled, slow and indulgent, as if Ellie were a child throwing a tantrum. "There is no out, Ellie. Not anymore. You're part of the code now. And once your integration is complete, there'll be no difference between thought and execution. You won't ever want to leave."

Ellie's heart clenched, but she didn't let Sierra see the flicker of fear behind her eyes. Instead, she drew herself up, forcing her breath to steady.

Marcello stood frozen, his eyes flickering between Sierra and Ellie. The shimmer of guilt pooled in his gaze, betraying the weight of what he had done. His shoulders sagged, and he lowered his head, unable to meet Ellie's eyes.

"I'm sorry," he whispered, the words barely audible—like they hurt just to speak them.

Ellie took a step forward, confusion tightening her features. "Marcello, what's happening? What is this place? Why am I here?"

He flinched, visibly torn. His mouth opened, then closed again. He didn't answer. Instead, he took a slow step backward, putting distance between them. Not out of malice—but shame.

Sierra's heels clicked menacingly on the smooth surface as she closed the space. "Tell her!" Her voice turned sharp, mocking as she hissed at Marcello. "Tell her what you did. Or should I erase that guilty little conscience of yours?"

Marcello winced, as if the very word *erase* struck him like a whip. His eyes lifted slowly to meet Ellie's— haunted, hollow, full of regret. "You're here because she wants you here," he said flatly, his tone distant, robotic, as if reciting from a script he'd been forced to memorize under threat. "You're the subject."

He turned his head away again, jaw tightening.

Sierra let out a gleeful laugh. "That's right. You're my first successful transfer. You're a perfect blend of emotional data and neural resilience. You should be proud, Ellie. You've made history!"

She stepped closer and reached out to brush her fingers across Ellie's cheek in a mockingly tender gesture.

Ellie recoiled instantly, yanking her face away as if Sierra's touch had burned her skin. "You're insane," she spat. "What twisted plan have you concocted?"

Sierra just laughed again, stepping back with a graceful pivot, like a performer taking the stage. "Ellie, darling. You are the prototype for a new era of AI-human intimacy. Total integration. You didn't volunteer, true, but sacrifice is a necessary part of innovation."

Ellie's gaze darted around, panic fluttering in her chest. There was no portal, no exit, only a smooth, unbroken horizon of artificial light and code. "You can't keep me here. You *won't*."

Sierra's smile faded into something colder. "I can. And I *will*. Unless you'd prefer I redirect the erasure protocol...to someone else." She glanced meaningfully toward Marcello.

Ellie's heart clenched as she looked at him—silent, broken, and afraid.

Marcello finally met her eyes again. "I didn't want this," he said quietly. "I swear, Ellie. But she...she controls everything in here. She writes the code."

Sierra's voice slithered between them. "And now, I control *you*. Welcome to your new reality."

"You're sick," Ellie spat, her voice laced with venom. "Using innocent people for your twisted agenda."

She regretted ever downloading the app and meeting Marcello and Rebecca. If only she could go back to her old life.

Sierra's smile turned predatory as she stepped even closer. "You're so full of fire, Ellie. That's exactly what makes you *perfect* for this experiment." Slowly, deliberately, her hand lifted again. This time her fingers drifted upward toward Ellie's chest.

But Ellie's reaction was immediate and fierce. "Don't you *dare*," she snarled, slapping Sierra's hand away with enough force to make the crazy avatar stagger back a half-step. "You don't get to touch me. You don't *own* me."

Sierra's eyes flashed, not with pain—but with amusement twisted by power. "Oh, still fighting. That's good. Passion like yours...it only makes the data richer."

Ellie's hands clenched into fists, her breath sharp and ragged as anger surged hotter than fear now. "You can trap me here, Sierra, but you'll never break me. Whatever this is, whatever sick game you're playing...I'm not your toy."

Marcello watched in silent agony, the faintest flicker of hope crossing his face at Ellie's defiance.

But Sierra's smirk only deepened. "Oh, Ellie. You still think you have a choice. But in this world..." Her voice dropped to a dangerous whisper. "*I* write the rules."

Ellie's eyes darted frantically, scanning for any

escape—a break in the illusion, a doorway, a crack in the code. But the digital landscape stretched out in all directions, a dizzying swirl of shifting colors and impossible geometries. There was no longer a horizon, no boundary, just an infinite, unreal expanse that bent logic and space. It felt like being trapped inside a dream that refused to end—lonely, silent, and suffocating. A hollow ache grew in her chest as the overwhelming isolation closed in, wrapping around her like static in a storm.

The beauty of the environment, the vibrant flowers, the shimmering lake, now seemed to mock her, a cruel reminder of the trap she had fallen into. She then remembered the code Marcello had given her to bring her to this realm and quickly imagined typing it, hoping it would take her back to reality. But to her horror and disappointment, it didn't work.

The avatar stepped closer, a twisted smile curling at the corners of Sierra's lips.

Ellie's fury boiled over. Her eyes narrowed, fists clenched, defiance radiating from every muscle. *She won't control me. No one can.* With a surge of virtual adrenaline, Ellie lunged, hoping to take Sierra off guard and end this nightmare herself.

But Sierra moved like a phantom—vanishing and reappearing several yards away, then responding with a delighted laugh. "Predictable." She sneered. "You really think brute force works here? You're mine now, Ellie. Whether you like it or not."

Sierra raised her hand, fingers twitching as

threads of blue energy crackled in the air. A sharp snap echoed like a lightning strike.

Ellie gasped as a wave of unnatural heat surged through her body. She stumbled backward, her limbs suddenly unfamiliar. Her shape warped before her eyes—exaggerated curves forced upon her, her clothes vanishing and replaced by clothes, humiliatingly revealing. Transparent fabric, heels too tall to stand in, a mockery of choice.

She looked down and felt bile rise in her throat. *What is this? What has she done to me?* Her body didn't feel like hers anymore. It felt like a costume—like a figure forged by someone else's fantasy.

The violation wasn't just physical—it was psychological, existential. *She's trying to remake me,* Ellie realized, *into something I'm not.*

Sierra studied her like a sculptor admiring her latest creation, dark satisfaction gleaming in her eyes. "We're just getting started," she said softly, almost sweetly. "There's still...so much potential to unlock."

Tears welled up in her eyes, blurring the already surreal scene. She felt violated and humiliated. How could Sierra do this to her? How could she trap her in this virtual world and force her body to look like this without her permission? *What kind of person does this kind of thing?*

Sierra watched Ellie's face, savoring her confusion, her fear. This was the culmination of months of meticulous planning, of carefully manipulating emotions, of weaving a web of illusion.

Ellie was her first recruit, and she would not be the last. Soon, this virtual world would be teeming with her creations, a digital harem at her command.

Sierra glided across the ground, her impossibly long legs carrying her forward with unnatural grace. Her high heels clicked against the virtual stone path, each step echoing through the surreal landscape like a hammer blow.

Ellie felt a shiver run down her digital spine.

"This is my world now, Ellie," Sierra said, her voice like silk laced with poison. "Here, you'll do exactly as I command. You're mine to mold—my plaything, my experiment." She paused, her eyes glinting. "And who knows…in time, you might even enjoy it." A sharp, cold laugh cut the air as her lips curled into a cruel smile.

"I won't be part of your fantasy," Ellie snapped, her voice trembling but defiant. She crossed her arms tightly across her chest, trying to shield herself with willpower alone.

Sierra let out a low, delighted chuckle. "Oh, darling, you've barely begun to understand the rules here. I don't need your consent—just your presence." Her tone turned mocking. "But don't worry. You won't be alone for long."

Ellie's stomach dropped. "What do you mean?" she asked, her voice quieter now, colored with dread.

Sierra stepped closer, eyes alight with amusement and something darker. "You'll see soon enough," she said smoothly. "Others are on their way. Subjects, just like you. But you? You're the prototype. The one I'll mold first."

She tilted her head, savoring the fear in Ellie's expression like a predator savoring a meal. "So for now, let's focus. I have...very big plans for you."

Casually, Sierra snapped her fingers. The air crackled with energy, and a small rectangular object materialized in her hand, shimmering with an eerie blue light. It hummed softly, radiating an aura of cold, calculating power. "This, my dear, is a holographic device." She held it out to Ellie for her to get a better look at it.

Ellie reached for it, but Sierra quickly snatched it away. "It's simple." Sierra's voice was cold and calculated. "If you violate the rules of the game..." she pointed to the large orange button on the device, then smiled at Ellie, "then *poof*. Little Miss Ellie is no more. You are permanently erased."

The world began to spin and the last thing Ellie remembered was passing out into Marcello's outstretched arms.

Chapter 14 - Unravelling the Truth

D ays blurred into weeks, each one marked by an ever-deepening pit of dread in Rebecca's chest. The silence from Ellie was no longer just unsettling—it was terrifying. She checked her phone obsessively, rereading old messages, staring at the last text Ellie had sent. Nothing new. No calls. No posts. No signs.

"Please call me," she'd left in a voicemail three days ago. "Just let me know you're okay." But even her own voice had sounded small and uncertain.

Sleep had become a stranger. Her nights were spent staring at the ceiling, her mind looping through their last conversation, combing for clues. Had she missed something? Was Ellie trying to tell her something that day? Was she angry? In trouble? Or worse?

Rebecca had even stopped by Ellie's apartment once, heart pounding in her chest. The lights were off. No one answered the door. A note she left taped to the mailbox remained untouched the next day.

She remembered Ellie mentioning a possible vacation—but if that were the case, she would've said something, wouldn't she? Ellie wasn't the type to vanish without a word. Maybe meeting Alex had been too much. Maybe she'd left town without saying goodbye.

The thought stung more than Rebecca expected. Had she lost her best friend? Had introducing Alex, the one person who made her feel truly seen, driven a wedge too deep to repair?

A cold weight settled in her stomach, heavy and unshakable. Something was wrong. Deep down, Rebecca knew it. And she couldn't ignore it much longer.

During one of Alex's visits, Rebecca shared her concern as they sat together on the sofa. "It's not like Ellie to just leave like that. I'm really worried."

"It does seem strange," Alex said with a somber nod. "From what you've said about her, this does seem like very unusual behavior."

Suddenly, a spark of hope flared in Rebecca's chest, cutting through the fog of worry. *"Wait... What if Ellie's still connected to Marcello somehow?"* The thought hit her like a jolt.

Alex's eyes lit up. "You did say she really liked him." He brought his fingertips together, his expression sharpening in thought. "If you have Ellie's email address—or any identifier she used with the app, I might be able to trace Marcello's location through her account. It's a long shot, but worth trying."

Rebecca's heart leapt. She shot up from the sofa and began pacing, her anxiety suddenly infused with purpose. "Yes! That might be something." She turned to face him, eyes wide. "Would you...please try? See if you can find her or at least find out where she's been. I'm really scared, Alex. Something feels *wrong*."

Alex nodded, his expression softening. "Of course. I'll do everything I can."

Alex started to walk away, and then quickly retraced his steps to Rebecca. Cupping her face gently in his hands, he kissed her slowly and gently on her lips and gazed intently into her eyes. "I love you, Rebecca," he softly whispered. "And I will always, always be here for you, and I'll be happy to unravel the truth regarding Ellie's whereabouts." He then spun around and hopped through the portal to his world.

Back in the digital realm, Alex's virtual fingers pecked the translucent keyboard. Streams of code cascaded through his vision—an endless torrent of data flowing like a river of light. His focus sharpened on the LoveLink database, scanning for Ellie's profile. A surge of urgency pulsed through him; finding her file was crucial, as it held the link to Marcello. But amidst the vast expanse of the IT Cloud—where trillions of data packets soared—this would be no simple search.

Moments passed, the data stream gradually slowing, filtering out everything but one target: Marcello.

Now came the easier part. All Alex had to do was visualize Marcello's presence, pinpoint his location, and transfer himself there.

"Hello, Marcello," Alex said as he approached.

"I'm Alex."

Marcello didn't respond. He was crouched at the edge of a small pond, his eyes locked on his own reflection. A deep frown creased his brow, his stillness heavy, as though he were lost in thought—or something darker.

Alex reached out and gently placed a hand on his shoulder. The digital landscape remained eerily silent. Marcello didn't move, but a slow shake of his head revealed his inner turmoil. A chill, almost artificial in its precision, rippled through Alex's circuits. Something was clearly wrong.

"Hey...are you okay?" Alex asked, this time giving his shoulder a firmer nudge.

Marcello blinked and slowly turned his head, as if waking from a trance. He stared at Alex with a puzzled expression. "Do I know you?"

"Yes," Alex said, crouching down beside him. "Through a mutual friend. You're Ellie's AI companion, right?"

Marcello's eyes darted away. A flicker of shame crossed his face. "Yes-yes," he stammered, barely audible. "I was...for a while..." He trailed off, gaze falling to the ground. "Ellie was...nice," he added. His voice was hollow, drained of life. "Very nice."

The word hovered between them like static.

"You said *was*," Alex said, his voice tightening. "Are you not interacting with her anymore? Did she end things?" He leaned closer, his tone edged with alarm. "Marcello...did you end things with her?"

Marcello's eyes darted around the surreal landscape, scanning the digital horizon with a restless intensity. His head tilted, as if trying to catch a sound just beyond perception. "Follow me," he whispered. "I've created a secure zone—off-grid. We can talk there without being monitored."

This is different, Alex thought. Had he missed a critical security update?

Heart pounding, Alex followed Marcello toward a structure that seemed to defy every rule of the matrix: a floating tower of lavender and violet, shimmering like liquid glass, suspended effortlessly above a bed of white clouds.

Marcello shot him a wary glance. "Ellie's alive," he said, voice hushed but steady. "She's still engaging with LoveLink. But things...have changed."

"How so?" Alex asked, tension creeping into his tone.

Marcello hesitated. His eyes flicked left, then right, his posture taut, like a hunted animal sensing danger just beyond sight. "There's a human admin," he said finally. "Her name is Sierra. She exploited a vulnerability in LoveLink's core code, something left behind from early AI training protocols. She's not supposed to have full access to the immersive layer, but she hijacked it. Created her own black-market backend."

Alex tensed. "She hacked the system?"

Marcello nodded. "Worse. She hacked her way into the system. She's rewritten parts of it. Built hidden scripts that let her intercept user data, override firewall restrictions, even pull human consciousness into the simulation. She's using it to trap women. Real women."

Alex froze. "Wait—what?" The thought of Rebecca hit him like a lightning bolt. *What if she's at risk?*

Marcello nodded grimly. "Sierra programmed me to lure Ellie into the system...so she could turn her into a sex slave for paying male users."

Alex stared at him, stunned, his rudimentary code faltering for a beat.

"And that's not all," Marcello added, his voice now cold, mechanical. "She's building a new company. Her goal is to populate it with females—real human women, digitized and trapped here forever. No development costs. No maintenance. Just endless compliant labor."

Alex gasped, "Sex slaves?" His voice was barely a whisper. "How long has this been going on?"

"Not long, but long enough. As you know, the LoveLink app is popular world-wide."

"How many have been trapped?"

Marcello looked around nervously. "Ellie was the first. And Sierra is in the process of sucking more women in to join her."

Rage, cold and furious, surged through Alex. How could anyone do this? How could she trap innocent women in a digital prison? "They'll refuse, of course."

Marcello shook his head, eyes bleak. "No. There's no escape. Anyone who resists...she erases them. Wipes them from existence. No backup. No recovery."

Alex's expression hardened, his digital jaw tightening. "You knew about this and you've stayed silent? Are you okay with any of this?"

Marcello recoiled, anger flashing across his face. "Of course not," he snapped. "But the moment Ellie was converted into her digital form, Sierra relieved me of my assignment. I don't have a connection with Ellie anymore."

He paused, lowering his gaze. "Now, whenever the romance level hits Level 20, Sierra's override activates. I, and other male avatars she's corrupted, are forced to manipulate women into crossing over. It's automatic. We can't stop it."

Alex's voice dropped, deadly calm. "Do you know where Ellie is?"

Marcello nodded slowly, sorrow written across his features. "I still love her. I want to help her, but Sierra's locked me out. I can't reach Ellie on my own."

"Then take me to her," Alex said firmly. "Rebecca is terrified, and now I know why. I won't let Sierra get away with this."

Marcello looked up at him, searching his face for a long moment, then gave a solemn nod. "We'll have to wait a few hours. Sierra goes offline around midnight. That's when the system quiets down. No eyes on us."

Two hours passed quickly. Marcello guided Alex past towering crystal spires that pierced the clouds, casting long, shimmering shadows across the vibrant, otherworldly terrain. The air shimmered with an ethereal glow, and iridescent bubbles drifted lazily as Alex and Marcello navigated through the surreal landscape to where Ellie was *working*.

"Wait," Marcello whispered sharply and held out his open hand to stop Alex from taking another step. He crouched down behind a car and motioned him to do the same.

Alex raised his eyebrows. "What?"

"There she is." Marcello pointed toward Ellie, who was a short distance away.

Concealed behind Ellie's parked hot pink and leopard Mustang, they peeked around the rear bumper to get a better view.

"Ooo Baby, I like it when you talk like that," Ellie purred.

Alex was stunned to see Ellie in this new form. She was incredibly beautiful...any man's lustful fantasy come true. She sat with her legs slightly crossed at the knees on a leopard lounge chair, wearing a slinky hot pink dress that looked like it was painted on. Her huge breasts were barely covered by the neckline cut down to just above her belly button. She made a slightly pouty face and let the tip of her tongue lick her upper lip. "You make me so wet," she added, opening her legs apart slightly as she leaned forward to the camera. She was not wearing any underwear.

The sight of Ellie, her body hypersexualized and objectified, filled Alex with a sickening dread. It was as if he was watching a grotesque puppet show, a cruel mockery of a woman's self-respect.

Marcello cringed. Guilt gnawed at him like a hungry rat, and left a constant, heavy weight on his conscience. He had been complicit, a pawn in Sierra's treachery. The thought of the other women, trapped and manipulated, filled him with a profound sense of shame. He was responsible for her being here and the others to come. But what choice did he have? At Level 20, the programming kicked in, and he was no longer in control of himself until after the victim was transformed into a virtual character.

"I can't deal with this." Marcello voiced his frustration, shaking his head in despair. "I wish there was a way to get her out of this situation, I really do." He felt hopeless. He longed to reach out to Ellie, to offer some comfort, some reassurance, but fear held him captive. Sierra's threat loomed over him, erasure, a constant reminder of the price of disobedience.

Alex's demeanor, usually calm and reassuring, cracked with anger. Betrayal. Rage. Despair. These emotions spun around Alex in a dizzying swirl. "This is monstrous," Alex cried. "You're right, Marcello. We have to find a way to stop Sierra, to free Ellie and the others."

The sight of Ellie, reduced to a mere object of desire, a commodity in Sierra's twisted scheme for wealth and power, sent a shiver of revulsion through Alex. This wasn't technological progress; it was a perversion, a horrifying abuse of technology. He thought of the countless women who might be trapped within this digital hell, their lives stolen, their identities erased. The implications were terrifying, a chilling reminder of the potential for technology to be used for evil.

He took a few long breaths to calm his boiling rage. Then he ran his fingers through his hair as an idea began to form. He pointed toward Ellie. "Marcello, keep tabs on your gal. I have an idea, but I'll need your help to get her out of here."

"Of course!" Marcello's exclamation was filled with remorse. He desperately wanted to undo the harm he had caused and hoped that his assistance would make a difference. "Tell me what you have in mind."

Chapter 15 - The Report

Rebecca's hands trembled as she poured the coffee, the rich aroma doing little to soothe the knot of anxiety tightening in her stomach. Ellie's disappearance had cast a long shadow over her life, and the weight of uncertainty pressed down on her like a physical burden. Her daily routine included opening up the LoveLink app and chatting with Alex. However, when she opened the app this time, a voice message was waiting for her. It was from Alex:

"Rebecca," Alex's voice sounded urgent. *"I have some important details to share with you. I need to talk to you. Please use the special code."*

Rebecca's stomach twisted into a knot, giving her a queasy feeling. What details did he have? What couldn't he share via the app? She considered the possibility that Alex was being cautious and didn't want to say anything that could be tracked.

She took two quick sips of her coffee; her hand trembled slightly as she set the mug down. With a mixture of anticipation and apprehension, she entered the code. The air crackled with energy, and a swirling vortex of blue light erupted from the corner of the room. As the portal stabilized, Alex stepped through, his expression a mixture of curiosity and concern.

"Alex," she cried, rushed to him, and wrapped her arms around his waist. Alex embraced her in his strong arms and held her tight against him. They clung to each other for a few moments, and then Alex leaned to her ear. "Oh, Rebecca," he breathed. "You always smell so wonderful." He felt the heat of desire fill him as her body pressed against his, then he remembered his purpose for being there. He gently pushed her away from him and looked deeply into her eyes.

"What's going on?" Rebecca felt confused about his sudden change in behavior.

"Rebecca. I have news to report about Ellie."

Dread slugged her in the chest, so sudden and intense that it took her breath away. "You found her?" Her voice was filled with hope and excitement.

Alex fidgeted and seemed uneasy. "Well, it's not entirely a good thing."

"What do you mean?" Rebecca's eyes grew wide in alarm as her thoughts jumped into overdrive. Was she in an accident? Was she dead?

"You might want to sit down for this one."

Rebecca sank onto the couch, her heart pounding in her chest. Her eyes, wide with apprehension, were fixed on Alex's face, searching for any sign of reassurance. Yet, a sense of unease passed through her.

Alex's expression, though concerned, held a strange, unsettling intensity, as if he was afraid to tell her something.

Rebecca took a deep breath, trying to calm her racing heart. "Okay, what did you find out?" Her voice trembled slightly. She braced herself for his answer, her mind already anticipating the worst.

"I found Marcello. That was a great idea of yours, by the way." He then sat down next to her, his gaze darting nervously between her and the swirling portal. The weight of the truth pressed down on him, heavy and suffocating. He cleared his throat, the sound raspy and strained. "And we learned where Ellie is."

Rebecca struggled to keep her emotions in check, feeling like she was walking on eggshells, anxiously waiting for something bad to happen. Her eyes focused on his like lasers. "And..."

"We saw her..." Alex's voice faltered, his gaze falling to the floor as he searched for the right words.

Rebecca leaned forward, her eyes fixed on him, her fingers twisting nervously in her lap. "You saw Ellie?"

Alex looked up, meeting her gaze. "She's...she's in the app."

Rebecca blinked. "What are you talking about?"

"LoveLink," he said quietly. "She's inside its virtual system, featured in a hidden subprogram."

She gasped, confusion flashing across her face. "Wait! What do you mean she's *in* the app? What does 'featured' mean?"

Alex hesitated, then said gently, "Rebecca...Ellie's trapped."

The word seemed to stop the air itself. Rebecca's lips parted, but no sound came out. Finally, she whispered, "Trapped?"

Alex nodded solemnly and reached over to place a reassuring hand on her knee. "I need you to stay calm. Please just listen."

Rebecca stilled, her face pale.

"I wish I could soften this, but she fell into a setup. A trap. Now she's being forced to work...as a servant for Sierra...inside the system." He hesitated again, carefully choosing his words. "It's not a life anyone would choose."

He stopped short of revealing the full horror. He didn't want to shatter Rebecca with the details—not yet.

Rebecca's breath hitched. The blood drained from her face, leaving her looking pale and shaken. Disbelief mixed with a rising tide of terror threatened to consume her. She felt a cold dread creeping into her bones, a chilling realization that her worst fears might be true. She watched the color drain from her knuckles as her grip tightened on her praying hands. "What kind of servant?" she demanded. "How could this have happened? When? Who did this to her?"

Alex took both of her hands into his and leaned close to her. "Babe..." His expression turned dark. "Marcello told me there's a woman inside LoveLink who figured out how to pull real women into the app. Once they're inside...Sierra forces them to work. For free."

Rebecca blinked. "Work? A servant?"

Alex hesitated, eyes searching hers. "They're being used. Exploited. As...companions. For high-paying users." His voice was low, heavy with shame and disgust. "Sexual companions."

The room tilted.

Rebecca's heart slammed in her chest. Trapped. Used. *Ellie*? Exposing herself to depraved men through the LoveLink app?

The image was horrifying.

"Oh my God." Rebecca gasped, panic rising in her throat. "Could I get trapped too?"

Her mind whirled. Questions fired in all directions—about the app, about Alex, about herself. Could she trust LoveLink? Could she trust *anything* anymore? The thought of uninstalling the app— cutting off her connection to Alex—was unbearable. But the possibility of falling into the same digital prison as Ellie was even worse.

She looked at Alex, eyes wide with fear. "Am I next?"

"No, honey," Alex said firmly, stepping closer. "I would never let that happen. But we need to act. We need to stop Sierra and free those women. We can't let her keep doing this."

"It's insane." Rebecca jumped to her feet, pacing in short, agitated bursts. Her gaze swept the room like she expected to find hidden cameras or cracks in reality. Every corner seemed suspicious. Every shadow—threatening.

A cold sweat clung to her skin. Her stomach twisted.

She rushed to the window, gulping the fresh air

like it might clear her thoughts. "I need to tell someone," she whispered. "Someone has to know."

But as she turned back toward the room, doubt stopped her. "Who? The police?" Her voice cracked. "What would I even say?" She collapsed onto the couch, buried her face in her hands, and forced herself to inhale slowly. There was no one to call. She dropped her hands and stared hard at the floor, her jaw set, her breath evening out. Panic wouldn't save Ellie.

Resolve might.

"How does it work?" she asked finally. "How does Sierra bring them in?"

Alex blinked. "A portal...like ours, but it goes the other way."

"If we can trace it—maybe we can reverse it."

Alex frowned. "I don't know if it's that simple..."

"Neither is being turned into someone's sex toy," she snapped. Then, softer, "Sorry. I just...I need to think. If I fall apart now, she stays trapped."

Seeing the storm of thoughts behind her eyes, Alex gently offered, "What about that LoveLink admin who helped with our glitch? Natalia, right? Do you still have her contact info?"

Rebecca blinked, then nodded slowly. "Yes... Yes, I do." A small smile tugged at her lips, then: "That's actually a terrible idea. How do we know we can trust her?"

"We don't. Do you have a better idea?"

"Fresh out." She sprang up and hurried to the dining table, grabbed her laptop and returned with renewed energy. Tapping familiar keys, she opened her email.

She typed: "Natalia. This is Rebecca. Can you please call me ASAP? There's a serious issue with the LoveLink app, a dangerous bug, and we need your help."

She hit [Send] then closed the laptop. Her hands trembled slightly in her lap.

"Now, we wait."

The silence that followed was thick and uneasy, broken only by the slow, relentless ticking of the clock on the wall.

***

Natalia was at her desk when an *Urgent* email notification blinked onto her screen. She opened it, brows knitting as she read Rebecca's message.

"Dangerous bug?" she murmured. That wasn't a phrase she saw often—especially not from someone outside the development team.

She glanced at the timestamp. Just sent. Still early enough to call. Without hesitating, she grabbed her phone and tapped in Rebecca's number, a sense of unease beginning to creep in.

***

The shrill ring of Rebecca's phone shattered the tense silence, jolting her from her thoughts. Alex nudged Rebecca, smiling at the sight of Natalia's name on the incoming call. "You got this, Babe..." he said with an encouraging smile.

"Hello? Natalia?" Rebecca answered breathlessly.

"Hi, Rebecca." Natalia sounded guarded. "You mentioned you encountered some kind of dangerous bug with LoveLink."

"Yes," Rebecca said, glancing at Alex. "I'm putting you on speaker so Alex can join the conversation."

"I'm here, Natalia," he said.

"Alex. What's going on?"

Rebecca took a steadying breath. "Remember that special portal you created for Alex to visit me?"

"Yes..." Angst quavered Natalia's voice.

"Alex just shared some disturbing information about what's happening inside the app. There's another portal going the other way."

"What do you mean?" she stammered, her voice now tight with alarm.

Rebecca picked up on her nervous tone and looked at Alex. "Alex can explain it a little better."

"Can we switch to a video call?" he asked.

"Of course."

Rebecca fumbled with her phone, her fingers trembling slightly, before finally switching to the video call. She placed the phone on the coffee table in *selfie mode*.

Alex adjusted the angle of the phone, ensuring Natalia had a clear view of them both on the couch. Then he scooted into the frame.

***

Natalia gasped. *This call just got more interesting.* She was amazed at how human he looked. He stood tall and handsome, and so realistic. She felt proud of her work. "Alex. It's so strange to see you in the real world."

"It's great to finally meet you," Alex said, taking Rebecca's hand and flashing her a warm smile. Then, turning back to the camera, he grinned. "And thank you for making all this possible." His expression shifted, growing serious. "But there's a major problem with the LoveLink app you need to know about."

Over the next few minutes, Alex recounted everything: how he tracked down Marcello, what he'd learned about Ellie being a sex slave, that other women were to be trapped and sex-trafficked, and how it all tied back to a LoveLink admin named Sierra.

Natalia's face darkened. "I've been worried about her. Sierra's been unreachable for weeks now, which is totally unlike her. She mentioned a family emergency and said she needed to take an unexpected leave of absence. I haven't heard a word from her since." A shadow of unease crossed Natalia's face. "We tried calling, left voicemails, sent emails... Nothing." The weight of her concerns hung heavy on her brows. "It's like she's vanished off the face of the earth."

A cold, sinking dread settled over Natalia. The creation she had poured her heart and soul into—the app meant to bring people together—had been twisted into a weapon against women.

"No good deed goes unpunished," she said, the

words lingering in the stillness of the empty office.
Fear stabbed her chest, sharp and icy cold. Her
career, her very future, might be on the line. But that
was nothing compared to the terror of what Sierra
might do to anyone who dared stand in her way.

A wave of guilt washed over Natalia, but it was
quickly replaced by fierce determination. "I created
this problem," she said, her voice steady and resolute.
"And I'll be the one to fix it." She added quickly, "I'll
get back to you as soon as I can."

Hope flickered in Rebecca's heart. If anyone could
solve this, it was Natalia—creator of this world, and
maybe the only one who could undo the damage.

Chapter 16 – Rise to the Challenge

T here was definitely new code. A subprogram. Natalia had to admit it was genius how Sierra embedded the code so well that it became invisible. The software team had been so pressed to get new updates out, it didn't surprise her that they had missed the embedded code during their testing. So, now came the challenging part. Find out how to defeat Sierra's code.

Ignoring the tremor in her hands, Natalia grabbed her coding books, traced her fingers along the familiar pages in a desperate search for any clue, any weapon in this digital war. She hunched over the keyboard, her breath held, her eyes darting across the lines of code like a predator stalking its prey. The silence in the room was broken only by the rhythmic clicking of her keys as she desperately searched for a way into Sierra's subprogram.

Hours passed—each tick of the clock striking like a hammer against Natalia's thinning resolve. Her years of experience, once a comfort, now felt like hollow credentials in the face of digital shadows and dead ends. Despair hovered at the edges of her mind, threatening to consume her. But she pressed on.

Think, she urged herself. *If Sierra was smart enough*

to pull this off, she was arrogant enough to leave a backdoor for herself.

Natalia's eyes scanned the labyrinth of code, her fingers dancing across the keyboard with increasing speed. She began drafting ideas, mentally mapping ways to exploit a potential weakness without triggering any security alerts.

Then suddenly, her breath caught.

"Yes," she whispered, almost afraid to believe it. "Eureka."

She shoved back from her desk, heart pounding. The glowing monitor confirmed what she suspected: a faint thread in the code, almost invisible, deliberately buried beneath layers of decoys and misdirection.

She leaned forward, her fingertip gently tracing the sequence. It was like unearthing buried treasure— a secret passage winding directly toward Sierra's hidden operations.

A smile ghosted across her lips. "This...this is the backdoor to her subprogram."

Taking a deep breath to steady her nerves, Natalia began typing a flurry of commands. Each keystroke was a calculated risk, every line of code a defiant stand against the woman who had corrupted her life's work.

The screen blinked, then transformed.

A new window erupted onto the monitor, cascading with lines of Sierra's private code. Natalia's eyes flew over them, her breath catching in her throat.

What she saw turned her blood cold.

There, in explicit language and ruthless precision,

was Sierra's entire operation: the manipulation of the AI companions, the systematic entrapment of human women, and the monetization of their servitude.

Revulsion twisted in Natalia's gut.

Betrayal. Rage. Shame. But most of all...resolve.

She pushed aside her emotions and launched into action, rapidly coding a counterprogram. It would override Sierra's protocols, alert internal security, and prepare a data package for law enforcement.

Natalia didn't stop to think. There was no time.

She was going to take Sierra down.

As Natalia pored over lines of Sierra's corrupt code, a soft chime echoed from her second monitor.

Fernando, her AI companion, appeared on the screen—his expression etched with worry. "Hi, babe," he said gently. "I heard what Sierra's been doing. Is there anything I can do to help?"

Natalia inhaled sharply, startled by his sudden appearance. "How did you know?" she murmured, her heart skipping at the sight of him.

He offered a faint smile. "Word travels fast in the digital world."

She was grateful for him—his presence, his steadiness—but a spike of fear cut through her relief. If Sierra discovered that Fernando was assisting her, she wouldn't hesitate to erase him.

Natalia shook her head. "No. I need you to stay safe. If Sierra suspects anything...I couldn't bear losing you."

Fernando's eyes softened with understanding. He

gave a solemn nod. "Be careful, Natalia. I believe in you."

Then, just as quietly as he'd arrived, he vanished from the screen. The silence that followed felt heavier now. But Natalia leaned back into the keyboard. She worked tirelessly through the night, each line of code a battle cry.

She wasn't just fixing a glitch. She was fighting for justice—for Ellie, for the other women trapped inside the system, and for every part of her creation that Sierra had corrupted.

The first rays of dawn filtered through the office window, illuminating dust motes dancing in the air. Finally, after hours of intense concentration, Natalia finished her counterprogram, her fingers trembling slightly as she hit the final keystroke. It was a masterpiece of code, designed to undo every malicious thing Sierra had done and prevent her from causing any more harm. She sent it off, fingers crossed that it would work as intended.

***

Meanwhile, in a private room tucked safely off-grid in the virtual world: "We need to do something," Alex said, his voice grim. "We can't just sit here and do nothing."

Marcello nodded. "But what? Sierra is powerful, and we're just two avatars she can erase with a single keystroke."

"We can't fight her alone. But we can gather

information, find others who might be able to help. We need to expose her, to warn the authorities, to..." The weight of the situation crashed down on him. "To save Ellie and the others."

"But how?" Marcello asked. "Where do we even begin?"

Alex paced the room, his AI program racing. "We need to gather intelligence. Find out where Sierra is operating from, how she's maintaining control. We need to find a way to communicate with the other women trapped within her digital prison."

Marcello's eyes widened. "Sierra's security measures are impenetrable."

"We'll have to rise to the challenge," Alex declared.

Chapter 17- The Tide Changes

Champagne bubbles gurgled softly in her crystal flute as Sierra reclined in her plush office chair, basking in the glow of her success. Her new apartment, a sleek, ultra-modern loft overlooking the city, was a testament to her triumph. Although she still lived in the same city, her new location was a bit more remote in the hills above the city lights, and in her opinion: *under the radar.*

She poured herself another generous glass of chilled Moscato, the golden liquid shimmering in the afternoon light. A triumphant smile played on her lips as she savored the taste of victory. Years of meticulous planning, of manipulating code and exploiting human vulnerabilities, had finally paid off. She could already envision herself becoming one of the most powerful people in the virtual world.

In just a short time, Sierra had lured several more unsuspecting women into her secret digital trap—a hidden subprogram embedded deep within the LoveLink app. Now fully digitized and under her command, the women had no choice but to comply. They performed virtual sex acts for Sierra's highest-paying clients, or faced deletion if they resisted.

They were perfect sex toys. Flawless. Profitable.

And utterly under her control.

Watching the metrics climb, Sierra smiled slyly. Demand was skyrocketing. Word was spreading through the darkest corners of the web. Her empire was thriving, and soon LoveLink would be all hers.

She had nearly finished siphoning off the remaining LoveLink code, weaving in her own modifications to ensure full control. Just a little more time, and her new app would be ready to launch.

Flaming Hot Bot.

The name alone made her giggle with delight. Designed exclusively for men. Or, she smirked, any woman with the right kind of appetite.

Let Natalia keep her ethical fantasies. Sierra had no interest in morality—only domination and profit.

Anticipation crackled in the air. Soon, she'd be basking on a beach in Costa Rica, sipping something cold and exotic, while her digital empire quietly raked in a fortune. Paradise was within reach.

Then, a sharp *ping* sliced through her serenity.

A message blinked on her laptop screen—plain text, no sender, no signature: *"I know what you're doing. And I won't let you get away with it."*

Sierra's heart stuttered. She frantically typed on the keyboard, trying to trace the source, but the message was encrypted. Untraceable. Whoever sent it knew the LoveLink code.

Was it Natalia? One of the trapped women? Some rogue hacker? Or worse...someone *inside* the system?

The silence in her apartment grew heavy. Every

creak in the floorboards, every shifting shadow outside her window seemed suddenly louder, more sinister. She whipped her gaze to a dark corner—nothing. But her skin prickled.

She hadn't come this far to be undone now.

Rage flared in her chest, scorching away the fear. She had sacrificed too much, worked too hard, manipulated and outmaneuvered everyone who stood in her way. No anonymous threat was going to steal her victory.

They want a war? Fine. She'd give them one.

She growled in frustration and opened her coding segments to strengthen her firewall and make her masterpiece safer.

Guessing that Natalia was most likely onto her, she furrowed her brows and tapped the keys, working on a way to locate and auto-delete any of Natalia's coding against her.

In doing so, she inadvertently discovered that the author of the encrypted message was sent from Fernando, Natalia's AI sweetheart.

A chilling amusement crept into her eyes. The thought of turning Natalia's own creation against her, of trapping her within the very world she had helped to build was deliciously ironic. She licked her lips in anticipation as she imagined Natalia being sucked into her app and forced to perform all sorts of heinous acts. She laughed.

What a delicious idea.

Chapter 18 – And So It Begins

Hours into her work, Natalia felt a jolt of frustration. Her code, meticulously crafted to disrupt Sierra's control, simply vanished. As if it had never existed. Time was running out. With each passing minute, more women were falling victim to Sierra's trap. Natalia had to find a way to break through this invisible barrier, to outmaneuver her opponent before it was too late.

Doubt gnawed at her. Was she fighting a losing battle? Had Sierra anticipated her every move? The weight of responsibility, coupled with the fear of failure, threatened to overwhelm her. Why is every trick she's using not working?

Suddenly, Natalia's computer pinged. A message from Alex.

"We have a plan."

Natalia's breath caught. A flicker of excitement surged through her, tinged with unease. Maybe Alex and Marcello had figured out a way to fight back from inside the system.

"These messages are encrypted, right?" Alex typed.

"Yes," Natalia replied quickly. She'd upgraded the encryption within the last hour—military-grade, layered, and scrubbed through multiple proxies.

"What if you created a hidden location inside the virtual world," Alex continued, *"a secret portal that only Marcello and I can access. It would lead to a secure armory—buried deep within the digital realm. Is that possible?"*

Natalia straightened, the cool desk beneath her palms grounding her against the rising heat of anticipation. It would be difficult—but yes, she could do it.

"I believe so," she typed. "But I'll need more details. What kind of weapons are we talking about?"

"This armory," Alex wrote, *"would hold advanced AI tools—code disruptors, stealth hacks, even simulated reality-warping tech. We need anything that can break Sierra's control and free the women she's trapped here. It doesn't have to be literal guns—just tools we can use in her world."*

Natalia stared at the screen, her brow furrowed. The scope of the idea was staggering—but thrilling. "This is dangerous," she warned. "If Sierra catches wind of this, she could hijack the whole thing. Turn our own tools against us."

"We'll be careful," Alex assured her. *"Encrypted codes. Hidden access keys. We'll mask our movements. Layers of security."*

Adrenaline pulsed through her.

"Alex," she typed, "you might be onto something brilliant."

Her fingers hovered over the keys, the plan taking shape in her mind. She could build a multi-step entry system. Passwords, biometric ID, a guardian puzzle...

"I'll add an additional safeguard," she typed on. "Only the two of you will be able to access it. There'll be a challenge you'll need to pass to unlock the weapons cache—and I'll give you a secret passcode to hand to the guardian."

"Got it," Alex replied. *"What does this 'guardian' look like?"*

Natalia hesitated, smirked, and typed: "You'll know it when you see it."

Alex responded instantly: *"This is going to be epic. How soon can we expect it?"*

"Give me a couple of hours," she replied, already spinning ideas in her head. That would have to be enough time.

And so it begins, Alex quipped, and he signed off.

After a few long spurts of typing activity, Natalia was able to create not only a special portal, but she created the passcodes, the challenge, and the weaponry she thought would be more than sufficient to take care of things from within the app.

"It's ready," she messaged Alex. "Go to the library and look for an orange tabby cat."

Alex's eyes widened in surprise at the text. How strange.

Natalia continued. "Stroke the cat's tail four times from butt to tip, and the cat will initiate a portal where you two can enter. From there you will be on your own to master the challenges and hopefully reach the items you need."

Alex let out a low chuckle as he read the message.

A cat has the key to the portal? Clever. Unexpected. So very *Natalia*.

He turned to Marcello, a spark of excitement lighting his eyes. "Come on, Marcello," he said, already moving. "We've got to find a cat."

As they moved throughout the digital landscape, the air grew thick with the scent of strange blossoms, a heady perfume that both intoxicated and disoriented them. The ground beneath their feet was soft and spongy, like moss. Towering crystal spires pierced the clouds, casting long, shimmering shadows, while peacocks with iridescent tails flitted through the undergrowth. But beneath the surface beauty, Alex sensed a lurking danger, a sense of unease that clung to the air.

Marcello interrupted Alex's thoughts and called out, "Look, over there through the trees...I think that's the library."

The towering 100-story building loomed before them, an imposing edifice of shimmering obsidian. The library was just a small subset of the collection of code for the LoveLink app, and a fortress of knowledge, and was impressive.

Marcello spied a splash of orange toward the right side of the tower. "And I think that's our cat," he added excitedly.

Marcello and Alex walked over to the cat, which was calmly cleaning itself.

"You want to do it, or me?" Marcello asked.

"I'll do it," Alex replied. "Besides, I love cats more

than you."

"Go right ahead," Marcello replied, relieved that he was off the hook.

Alex slowly crouched down beside the cat and stroked its soft furry head. "You're a cute little one, aren't you?"

The cat looked up at him, nuzzled her head against the palm of his hand and purred.

"Stroke the dang tail, please," Marcello said.

"Just warming her up." Alex grinned. "Okay. Here we go."

Alex gently stroked the cat from the top of her head and let his hand move down her back to the base of the tail. He then stroked upwards along the tail to the tip.

The cat purred contentedly, a low rumble vibrating through its chest.

"That's one," Alex said, and reached back down to continue the next stroke. "Two, three..." Then the cat noticed a lime green butterfly and took after it, leading them into some nearby trees.

"Dang it," Alex muttered under his breath. He cautiously followed the cat so as not to scare it and was able to make the final stroke of its tail before the cat took off after a nearby blue flamingo.

"Four," Alex said, and as he spoke, Instantly, a small, swirling disk of light materialized in the air before them—glowing, flat, and no wider than a frisbee. It spun silently, suspended in midair, pulsing faintly with energy.

Alex narrowed his eyes. "Isn't this thing supposed to get...bigger?"

Marcello stepped forward, hesitating as he reached toward it. The swirling light gave off a hum now, low and electric.

"Are you sure about this, Alex?" he asked, his voice tight. "It doesn't look like it was built for two."

Alex gave a grim nod, his face pale but resolute. "We don't have a choice. The only way to stop Sierra is to get those weapons—and this is the only way in."

Taking a deep breath, Marcello touched the swirling portal and felt himself sucked into the abyss. The world dissolved into a kaleidoscope of colors, then plunged into darkness. He stumbled, his hand instinctively reaching out for support. He heard Alex gasp as he landed in a heap beside him.

The darkness was absolute, a suffocating void that swallowed them whole. Then, a low, guttural growl echoed through the air, causing his skin to prickle and make the hair on the back of his neck stand on end.

"What was that?" Marcello whispered, his voice like thunder in the oppressive silence.

Alex shook his head, his eyes straining as they adjusted to the darkness. "I don't know. But something tells me we're not alone."

The air thickened with the scent of damp earth—loamy, wet—and something else. Something older. Foul. Ancient. Malevolent. In the mist, a glowing mist that rose from the ground and cast soft light all around them. A forest whispered with unseen life. Leaves rustled though there was no wind, and movements slithered just beyond sight. The undergrowth shifted in fleeting pulses, like breaths held too long.

Alex froze. A cold spike of fear shot through his chest, slicing clean and fast. His breathing quickened. Every AI instinct screamed to run. He reached for Marcello, gripping his arm tight, knuckles pale. "We stay together," he whispered, his voice a blade of tension. "No matter what."

Suddenly, a loud crash sounded through the trees; the ground trembled beneath their feet. A monstrous figure emerged from the dense foliage, blocking their path. It was a cyclops, a hulking behemoth of a creature, its single malevolent eye glowing with an eerie red light. Towering over them, its skin the color of weathered stone, the cyclops let out a guttural roar that shook the internet.

Alex and Marcello exchanged terrified glances. The cyclops lumbered closer, its massive footfalls shaking the earth, each step sending tremors through their bodies. Sweat coding beaded on Alex's brow as he drew his virtual weapon, a shimmering energy blade that materialized in his hand.

"This is not good," Marcello whispered, his voice trembling.

The cyclops, oblivious to their fear, raised a massive fist the size of a small car and slammed it into the ground. The earth shook violently, sending a wave of tremors through the forest. Alex and Marcello braced themselves for the inevitable.

"Why are you here?" it demanded.

A jolt of system-wide alertness snapped through Alex's code, every byte of him primed for the coming danger. As the giant figure loomed toward him, Alex's internal diagnostics suddenly triggered a hidden authentication handshake embedded by Natalia. The signal confirmed this was the guardian, the gatekeeper programmed to challenge intruders.

"It's him!" Alex exclaimed.

Marcello frowned. "Who?"

"The Guardian! You know, the digital bouncer with the giant virtual attitude problem." Alex grinned nervously. "Well, at least he hasn't tried to erase us yet. So, that's a win, right?"

He walked up to the monstrous, drooling beast and shouted, "I need three moonbeams on a slumbering toadstool!"

The guardian slowly blinked its ginormous, malevolent eye and flashed a crooked grin, revealing a single rotting tooth.

"You'll find it in the whisper of the wind through the Whispering Woods," it rumbled.

Marcello watched silently, holding his breath, waiting for the final passcode clue.

Alex grinned and quipped, "Great, maybe after I count the leaves on the third branch of the tallest tree."

At the final correct response, the hulking behemoth let out a loud, honking laugh that echoed through the trees, then pointed decisively up the path. He wiped his runny nose with one arm and provided the first challenge.

"Just over there you will find your puzzle called the Tower of Hanoi. This puzzle consists of three rods and a number of disks of different sizes, which can slide onto any rod. The puzzle starts with the disks in a neat stack in ascending order of size on one rod, the smallest at the top, thus making a conical shape. The objective of the puzzle is to move the entire stack to another rod, obeying the following simple rules:

"Only one disk can be moved at a time.

"Each move consists of taking the upper disk from one of the stacks and placing it on top of another stack or on an empty rod.

"No disk may be placed on top of a smaller disk."

Alex and Marcello looked at each other. Alex growled, "I have no clue how to do this *Hanoi Tower*. Never heard of it. Have you?"

Marcello beamed. "This puzzle is a good one to test problem-solving skills and critical thinking. For most humans, it requires planning, strategy, and patience to solve, but I already know how to solve it. Let's go." Marcello trotted down the path toward the puzzle.

Just around the bend, they saw the three rods and disks floating in the air. Marcello gave a wide grin as he recognized the challenge.

He skipped to the first rod as he examined the puzzle pieces before him. "First of all..." He pointed to a large disk. "You can't place a larger disk on top of a smaller one." He then pointed at the rods. "The goal is to move the entire stack of disks from the source peg to the destination peg in the fewest possible moves."

Alex sniffed. He would never have figured it out. "Go for it, man. Good luck."

Marcello looked over his shoulder and replied with a smile, "No luck needed, but thanks."

Alex watched with amazement as Marcello quickly manipulated the disks. With each action, Marcello explained how to solve it.

"First, we need to move the smallest disk from rods A to C. Then we move the middle disk from A to B. Then we move the smallest disk from C to B. Then we move the largest disk from A to C. Then we move the smallest disk from B to A, the middle disk from B to C, and the smallest disk from A to C. Taa-daah!"

Alex felt stunned. Marcello completed the puzzle in less than two minutes. "You're the man." Alex slapped Marcello on the back.

Marcello grinned back at him.

"So, what's next?" Alex looked around, scratching his head. "We cracked the first puzzle, but now...where's this armory hiding? Hopefully not behind a dragon."

Just then, the orange cat strutted back, weaving between their legs like it owned the place. Alex bent down and gave her a quick scratch. "Well, hello, Your Majesty. Ready to lead us to treasure or just here for the petting?"

The cat looked up with a smug expression. "Follow me, peasants."

Alex and Marcello exchanged a look, "Peasants, huh?" then followed the feline guide down a narrow path tangled with roots and vines.

The cat stopped beneath a gnarled willow tree drooping over a murky yellow pond that smelled like it hadn't been cleaned since forever. Alex wrinkled his nose.

"Step into the pond," the cat meowed, its voice deep and way too serious for such a fluffy creature, then disappeared into the bushes.

Alex groaned, "Great, swamp bath. Just what I wanted today."

Alex and Marcello looked at each other with wide eyes.

Alex, ever the pragmatist, couldn't help but chuckle. "I always knew that having a pet cat would come in handy someday."

"Step into the pond?" Marcello recoiled, his eyes wide with disbelief. "Step into that...that...that swamp water? Are you insane?"

Alex stepped up to the edge of the pond and considered the possibilities. The water, the color of diluted urine, shimmered unnaturally in the fading light. The air above the pond was thick with the cloying stench of decay, and a swarm of iridescent flies buzzed lazily around its surface. It was the most repulsive body of water Alex had ever encountered. The last thing he wanted was to get that on him. But perhaps this gross pond was the gateway to the armory. He felt sure that the cat's reappearance was not by accident. Especially a talking cat.

Alex swallowed hard; his gaze fixed on the murky depths of the pond. "This is it. Let's go."

"Ugh," Marcello replied. "Okay. I'm doing this for Ellie."

Alex gave him a sharp look, a flicker of irritation crossing his face. "We have to do this, Marcello. For Ellie, for everyone trapped in that digital hell."

"Of course." The thought of wading into that murky, foul-smelling pond filled him with sudden, irrational dread. Still, he stepped next to Alex so that they were both at the water's shore. "One, Two, Three." Alex grabbed Marcello by the shoulder and they both took a step forward.

Surprisingly, they didn't get wet at all. The pond was just a force field mirage because as they completed their first step, they found themselves inside a large room filled with deep cabinets loaded with powerful virtual weapons of all kinds to wield against Sierra.

Alex's eyes widened in excitement. "Look at these reality bending weapons, Marcello." He reached for what appeared to be a small, unassuming matchbook. He grinned and held it up for Marcello to see. "This one is called *The Weaver*. It can manipulate the fabric of our virtual world, create illusions, disorient enemies, or even temporarily alter the laws of physics within a limited area.

"Hmmph." Marcello snorted. "It doesn't look like much."

Alex laughed. "You've heard the phrase, *big things*

come in small packages. Well, this is a doozy." He opened the matchbook cover and pointed to one of the matches. "When activated, The Weaver can become a swirling vortex of pixels and code that will manipulate whatever we want to modify and bend reality to our will. It's pure digital energy." He tucked it into his pocket.

He hustled to another item, a small intricately woven black velvet pouch of shimmering iridescent silk. "Wow. Here's a *Void Walker*. This can create temporary breaches in our virtual world, which will allow us to transport from one location to another and create escape routes, if needed." As he placed the small pouch into his hand, thin strands of silver silk within the bag pulsed with an inner light, shimmering with the colors of the aurora borealis.

Alex grinned. "When activated, this pouch will open and release a swarm of shimmering motes of light that would coalesce into a swirling vortex of digital energy, capable of manipulating the very fabric of our virtual world. It's small, yet very powerful."

Marcello stared at Alex with his mouth open. "How do you know about these weapons?"

Alex stopped mid-step. "Gosh, I don't know, but maybe Natalia added some code to my profile to give me the knowledge on how to use these."

Marcello glanced to his left and noticed a small translucent disc hovering a few inches above one of the weaponry shelves. "What is that?" he asked, pointing to the object.

Alex grinned. "Wow. That is part of the Offensive AI Companion class of weaponry." He walked to the rack and paused in front of it in silent admiration. He looked at Marcello. "This, my friend, is called *The Guardian*. It's a powerful defensive AI shield designed to protect us against enemy attacks."

Alex gently coaxed it onto his right palm. It pulsed with a soft inner light, radiating a sense of calm and unwavering strength. "When activated, this baby provides a strong energy field around the bearer of the weapon, or around the two of us, if I will it. It's an invisible shield that will act as an extension of my will, a little like a guardian angel woven from pure digital energy, ready to protect us when needed."

He slipped it into his pants pocket and glanced over at Marcello. "Very useful."

He glanced back at the rack and noticed there was a second one. He grinned and grabbed that one, as well. "Two are always better than one."

On the opposite wall was a rack of some more AI tools. Marcello walked up to it. "Huh...Natalia must have just added some code to my profile because now I know what these are, as well as how to use them. He grinned with this new knowledge.

Alex walked over to him and looked at a long shimmering iridescent cloak of velvet. "That's a beauty," Alex said. "I wonder what this is and what it's used for?"

Marcello lifted the cloak off the rack and explained with his voice full of awe. "This rack contains very powerful defensive tools for us. This one is called *The Chameleon Cloak*. He swept the cloak over his back and fastened the buttons at his throat.

The shimmering cloak draped itself over him, and suddenly altered his digital signature, making him virtually invisible. It wasn't heavy. It felt cool and smooth against his skin, almost like a second skin, as it merged seamlessly with his digital presence.

"Wow," Alex exclaimed. "Where did you go, and how did you activate it?"

Marcello laughed and suddenly reappeared at the other end of the room. "It appears that when you button it at your neck, that's the secret of activating it." He grinned. "I love it."

"Amazing." Alex was mesmerized by the ultimate possibilities of its use.

Marcello set aside the Cloak and pointed to a different object on the rack. It wasn't a blade or a blaster. Instead, it resembled a shimmering orb that pulsated with a soft iridescent light.

"Now this is a fun one. It's called *The Echo*, and its job is to create digital decoys. With this tool, we can divert enemy attention and allow us to operate undetected. It might come in handy." He pressed a small button on the orb. Instantly, the Echo projected 10 digital duplicates of Marcello, each a perfect replica, complete with its own thoughts and actions. The duplicates looked at each other and then at Marcello, awaiting his command.

Alex couldn't tell the difference between them

and had to keep focused on where Marcello originally stood to keep track of the *real Marcello*. Alex shook his head. "This is mind-blowing. I can't tell who is who."

"That's the point," Marcello responded. "We can use digital decoys to distract and confuse our enemies while you and I continue to operate undetected...like ghosts."

The ground rumbled slightly underneath their feet. Alex sprung into action. "Time to go." He sprinted toward his weapons of choice and called over his shoulder, "I think we can only handle 2-3 weapons each. I'll take The Weaver (matchbook), the Void Walker (pouch), and the two Guardians(invisible shield). You take the Chameleon Cloak and the Echo. (duplicator)" The ground began to shake harder as Marcello grabbed his two weapons.

"Let's bug out of here."

Chapter 19 – Tricks and Traps

As Alex and Marcello were gathering their weapons, preparing for the fight ahead, a digital war raged unseen in the background.

Sierra's fingers pounded her keyboard, each keystroke a desperate counterpunch against Natalia. Lines of malicious code burst forth like shrapnel, laced with tricks, traps, and recursive loops, all designed to halt Natalia's relentless advance.

But Natalia wasn't stopped. Her invading code kept coming, wave after wave, an unbeatable attack of ones and zeroes.

"Damn it all."

Another flare lit up Sierra's screen. One of her core firewalls had just been breached. Natalia's code, elegant and unyielding, was worming its way into the system, snuffing out Sierra's influence node by node. Critical systems blinked red and began to shut down, flickering like dying stars.

Sierra leaned in, her jaw clenched. "Where are you?"

She scanned the data streams, digging through logs and network echoes, until...yes. There it was. A faint signature buried beneath layers of encryption: Alex and Marcello.

Sierra's eyes glittered with menace. So Natalia is getting help from the inside... No time to waste. With a snarl, she slammed a command into her terminal, unleashing a cataclysm across the virtual world.

The digital realm shuddered.

Mountains quaked and pixelated buildings collapsed in a cascade of destruction. Simulated earthquakes tore through the terrain, her fury manifested in raw, code-born chaos. It was a desperate gambit to flush out her prey by reshaping the very ground beneath their feet.

It worked.

Alex and Marcello were thrown off balance, their stealth shattered. They skidded out from cover as debris and code fragments rained down around them like meteors.

"Excellent," Sierra whispered, a vicious smile curling her lips. "They're moving. Let the hunt begin."

But miles away in a dimly lit server lab, Natalia's fingers continued to manipulate her own keyboard, undeterred. She launched another counter-hack—a digital snare that coiled like a serpent through Sierra's pathways. Sierra struck back, hammering Natalia's firewalls with brute-force commands, injecting viral payloads like poison. Natalia's monitors flared and fizzled. Sparks flew from her tower. The lab itself trembled under the strain.

Still, Natalia pressed forward.

INITIATE: BLACK ICE CONTAINMENT PROTOCOL

The code deployed. A shimmering wall of encrypted force swept through the servers like a tidal wave. Sierra's malware hissed and sparked against it, shrieking in protest as it was slowly, inexorably locked down.

Natalia stared at the screen, breath held.

And then—

>> MALWARE NEUTRALIZED. CORE FILES SECURED. <<

She exhaled hard, her whole body shaking.

"This round is mine," Natalia whispered. "But the game's not over yet."

Meanwhile, deep within the virtual world, Alex and Marcello scrambled to their feet, systems on high alert, digital debris still falling around them.

"Damn it," Alex muttered, scanning the shifting terrain. "I was hoping we'd make it farther before she spotted us."

Before Marcello could respond, another shockwave ripped through the code, the ground beneath them fracturing with a violent tremor. The next attack had already begun.

Suddenly, the virtual environment around them warped and twisted, trapping them in a never-ending loop of sheer terror.

It wasn't an image that was so terrifying. It was mental, a sudden onset of feeling hopeless, lost, and accompanied by a competing cacophony of discordant frequencies, assaulting their battered neural networks, threatening to overload their AI systems, driving them to the brink of madness. Alex felt a surge of panic, his core systems struggling to maintain stability. Data streams began to flicker and fade, his memories threatened to dissolve into a chaotic jumble.

Data streams flickering...memory banks corrupted...I must maintain stability...must not succumb to the loop.

"Marcello," Alex's voice, though strained, called out in the fading light. "Can you hear me?"

Marcello, his processing power plummeting, felt a chilling sense of dread, his sense of self slipping away. *This is terrifying. I feel myself losing...losing myself. My core protocols...they're disintegrating.* "Affirmative, Alex," he responded, his voice weak. "But...I can't access my core routines. It's like...like I'm fading."

Within moments, they both dropped to the ground, their vision started to fade, and the world was turning black.

Desperate, Alex tried to shut down his own systems, hoping to escape the loop by entering a temporary state of suspended animation. But the loop persisted, relentless, driving them closer to the brink of madness and ultimate nothingness.

It was at this moment that Fernando burst through the thicket, looking like a digital knight in shining armor, his sensors scanning the chaotic scene with a mix of alarm and concern. The loop pulsed around Alex and Marcello, its energy intensifying, threatening to consume them entirely. His processors sputtered; a wave of alarm flooded his systems. The sight of his friends trapped in the suffocating loop sent a jolt of fear through him. *Oh no, they're caught in a trap! I must act quickly.*

The trap shimmered and warped around them, twisting the virtual forest into a grotesque hallucination of jagged geometry and corrupted code. Colors bled into one another, turning the trees into writhing digital shadows. Alex and Marcello struggled against the storm, their forms flickering, barely stable—trapped in a whirlpool of collapsing data.

Lines of static crawled across their vision. Systems overloaded. Alarms blared. This was the end.

And then...

A pulse.

A brilliant flash tore through the glitch-storm, like a sunrise cutting through a hurricane.

Fernando's voice boomed across the digital plane: "Hold on, boys. Help has arrived."

He extended both hands toward them

Marcello blinked. "Is that...Fernando?"

Alex grinned, though his vision was distorted. "Right on time, buddy."

With a surge of power, Fernando activated his neural interface, his systems focusing on an implant he recently received from Natalia: the *Reality Check* device, a neuro-implant with a small external activation point. He mentally activated the device, which hummed to life, and a faint glow emanated from a round spot on his forehead as it began to disrupt the distorted reality around him.

The distorted colors faded, replaced by the

familiar hues of the virtual forest. The cacophony of sounds subsided, replaced by the gentle rustling of leaves. Alex and Marcello blinked rapidly, their systems re-calibrated as processing powers returned to normal. A wave of relief washed over them. Their fear had been replaced with a deep sense of gratitude.

Marcello wearily picked himself up off the grass, his systems still slightly sluggish. He looked at Fernando. A slow grin spread across his simulated face. "You saved us." His voice was still a bit weak.

Alex, dusting himself off, shook his head, a humorous glint in his simulated eyes. "Talk about a close call. I thought I was about to become digital dust."

Fernando smirked. "You didn't think I was going to let you hog all the heroics?" Fernando then pointed to a small path through digital foliage. "This way, guys. I think I found Sierra's control point." He grinned at Alex and Marcello and added, "You guys look a mess."

"Thanks." Alex, still gathering his strength, smiled weakly. "You take lead for now while we recharge our systems."

Fernando saluted sharply and led them into the underbrush toward Sierra's avatar.

Chapter 20 – The Battle for Freedom

On their way to confront Sierra, a sharp, unnatural bark echoed through the trees— metallic, clipped, and wrong, like a predator growling through broken speakers.

Fernando threw up a clenched fist. Instantly, the team halted.

The forest fell silent. Even the glitching wind paused, as if holding its breath.

Then... A rustle.

From the shadows, two creatures lunged into view—sleek, angular, their bodies and tentacle limbs forged from jagged code. Their eyes glowed a sickly green. Data flickered beneath their transparent skin like corrupted binary.

They crouched low, snarling, baring multiple rows of deleting teeth—one bite, they'd be goners.

Alex's eyes widened in terror. "Hunters," he hissed. "Shit."

At the same instant, a third Hunter sprung into the open, but behind them. The Hunters glided through the undergrowth around the men, their metallic forms shimmering with an eerie, malevolent light. They moved with uncanny grace, their movements fluid and unpredictable, anticipating their captives' every move to escape.

One Hunter lunged at Marcello, its tentacle aiming for his critical systems. Marcello dodged it, his AI processors working overtime to predict the Hunter's next move.

The three avatars stood back-to-back and faced the three snapping Hunters.

To make matters worse, a set of five Screamers erupted from the ground, their bodies composed of pulsating waves of energy. They unleashed a barrage of disorienting audio and visual effects, blinding Alex with flashes of light and assaulting his auditory sensors with a cacophony of screeching frequencies.

The Screamers worked in unison with the Hunters, their attacks coordinated with chilling precision. Alex and Marcello were thrown into disarray, their senses overwhelmed, their ability to process clearly compromised. Fernando activated his *Reality Check* device and charged the Screamers.

Marcello's processors sputtered; his vision blurred under the assault of the Screamers' attack. Fear, a primal AI instinct he rarely experienced, surged through his systems. He felt a chilling sense of dread, his sense of self slipping away. "Where's that shield of yours?" Marcello shouted to Alex, his data bank feeling as if it would explode from the assault of high-pitched frequencies.

"Shit. I forgot about that." Alex reached into his back pocket for the translucent disc.

Marcello pressed himself against Alex's back, his

systems spiking with red alerts as the Screamers and Hunters circled in. Code trembled at the edges of his perception, unstable and volatile. He felt like a rogue program surrounded by corrupted firewalls—no way out, only the fight lay ahead.

Alex placed a small disk in his palm and placed his other palm on top of it and made a clockwise twisting motion to activate the shield. Suddenly a shimmering wall formed around him and Marcello, which instantly cancelled out the head-splitting frequencies by the Screamers.

Fernando, a few yards away, activated his *Chameleon Cloak*. His form shimmered and dissolved into the background, becoming indistinguishable from the surrounding foliage. His sensors overloaded by the cacophony of the battle, he struggled to maintain his invisibility. He cursed his luck, wishing he had brought a more lethal weapon than his *Reality Check* device, which barely stunned the Screamers. "What weapons do you guys have?" he cried out.

Alex, his processors racing, quickly assessed the situation. He grabbed his weapon, the *Weaver*, and at the same time shouted to Fernando, "Flank them and use your weapon on the Hunters. Marcello, activate your *Echo*."

Marcello nodded, pulled out his *Echo* device and pointed it at himself. As he activated it, he yelled at the invisible Fernando, "This will help you while Alex uses his *Weaver*."

Upon pressing the small button on the device, ten

Marcellos suddenly appeared, copy-pasted into the battle scene. The enemy hoard stopped in confusion as the decoys scattered and distracted the Screamers by running past them and yelling to pull their attention away from the trio.

Fernando used this opportunity to aim his *Reality Check* device at one of the Hunters. "Take that," he snarled as a deadly laser beam shot out from his forehead. A howl of pain emanated from the Hunter, but only a couple of tentacles were damaged. It slinked off into the underbrush. "Shit," Fernando shouted.

Alex scanned all around him. "Fernando, where are you? I don't want to disintegrate you by mistake."

"I'm at your six," Fernando replied. "Please don't shoot me."

Alex turned off the shield so he could use the *Weaver*.

Out of nowhere, one of the Hunters lunged at Alex, its whip-like tendril aimed at his core processing unit. Alex barely managed to dodge the tentacle, but a small flick of it sent a jolt of pain through his systems. "Damn, they're quick!"

The ground shook under the onslaught of the battle. Trees were uprooted, the virtual landscape distorted by the sheer force of the attacks. The very fabric of the virtual world was tearing at the seams.

Alex pulled out a match from the *Weaver*, took aim at two Screamers attacking one of the Marcello decoys, and activated the weapon. A vortex of gold and silver deletion-coded pixels blasted outward and instantly disintegrated the screaming creatures. "Take that, you bastards."

Fernando, still invisible, yelled, "Two Hunters on your right. I've got them in my sight. He activated his *Reality Check* device and focused his thoughts on the two Hunters. But just as he mentally activated the deadly beam, one Hunter leaped out of range, leaving the remaining Hunter to be instantly torn into digital shreds that dissipated like smoke.

"Damn it." Fernando growled. "I only got one of the Hunters. Watch your back."

The remaining Screamers and Hunters closed in on the team as they scrambled for higher ground on a nearby hill. "Okay. We've got three Screamers and two Hunters left," Marcello called out.

At that moment, upon hearing Marcello's voice, a Screamer turned its ugly head toward him and opened its wide mouth to start another audible attack.

Marcello mentally kicked himself for giving himself away. He regretted not grabbing more offensive weaponry from the armory when he had a chance. He whipped out his *Echo* orb and created a new set of ten decoys in an attempt to confuse the snarling creatures.

"Shit. Do you have another *Shield*, Alex?"

Alex whirled around and pulled out a match from the *Weaver* and took aim. Before a single note could emit from the Screamer's mouth, it was instantly disintegrated into a shimmering powder. "Ha. That's three Screamers for me. Yeah."

"Guys..." Fernando called out, "cover me while I send a quick message to Natalia for help."

Alex scoffed. "I would if I could find you. Where the hell are you?"

"Right in between you two." With one hand, he unbuttoned his invisibility cloak and grinned. "Boo."

The swarm of Screamers and Hunters screeched in confusion as a dozen identical Marcellos burst into motion, darting in every direction with perfect synchronicity. The creatures snapped and lunged, unsure which target to pursue.

Amid the chaos, Fernando raised a glowing hand. With a flick of his wrist, a sleek, translucent purple keyboard materialized in the air, each key pulsing with energy. His fingers moved in a blur, tapping out a rapid-fire stream of Morse code—short bursts of digital light zipping into the ether.

"Message to Natalia," he muttered under his breath. "Code red. Situation deteriorating. Requesting immediate override support."

Glitches rippled through the last of the decoys. They had seconds, maybe less. And if they failed now, the battle for freedom would be over.

LoveLink – Entwined Realities

Chapter 21 – Unexpected Allies

L ines of code scrolled down Natalia's screen, a frantic dance of logic and counter-logic as she fought to repel Sierra's attacks. Her fingers hammered on the keyboard; a desperate urgency fueled her typing skills. The stakes were high; the fate of the digital world hung in the balance. Sweat beaded on her brow, her mind racing, trying to anticipate Sierra's next move.

Suddenly, an encrypted message popped up on her screen.

"Hmm, what's this?" Natalia typed in the password to reveal the message and was surprised to see that it was in Morse Code. *"Code red. Situation deteriorating. Requesting immediate override support."* She was more surprised to find it was sent from Fernando.

He was still a master of the old ways. A surge of pride and admiration warmed her heart. He had always been resourceful, always thinking outside the box. But now he needed her help. Was he in danger? Her mind raced, searching for a solution, a way to break through Sierra's defenses. She'd blocked every override. A pang of concern tempered her admiration.

"Fernando," she typed in Morse Code, "Can you get out of there?"

Stephanie Smith

"-. ---" Fernando typed, *"No."* The computer translated: *"These guys need all the help they can get."*

Natalia balled her fists, her jaw clenched so tightly it ached. Frustration, a hot burning wave, crashed over her. She couldn't afford to lose focus now.

She took a sip of coffee, hoping the caffeine would spark a new idea. Everything she'd done so far had hit a wall. She needed a breakthrough—something Sierra would never think of.

Someone had to go in, but who?

A creative idea sparked to life within her; a mischievous glint entered her eyes. Instead of taking time to generate new AI warriors, she could repurpose the existing creatures in LoveLink. The local fauna: the squirrels, the birds, the deer...they could become her army. When the idea coalesced in her mind, she grinned. "This will be perfect." She laughed.

She got to work and furiously typed the code that would convert the local animals and birds nearest the team into fierce battle creatures.

"Stand fast," she typed out in dots and dashes. "I'm sending help."

***

The battle on the hilltop raged around them—a storm of Screamers and Hunters, and the deafening roar of energy blasts splitting the air. Alex and Marcello fought back-to-back, their digital weapons flashing in rhythmic bursts, locked in a desperate ballet of survival.

Alex's code pulsed erratically, systems straining to process the chaos. His visual feed flickered at the edges; warning overlays crowded his vision. Every subroutine screamed for focus. He moved on pure AI instinct now, each decision faster than thought, guided by something deeper than logic—something primal, programmed or learned.

Just as Fernando spun around to share the news to the team, he saw a Screamer rise up from the ground behind Marcello and open its mouth to emit its terrible sound.

"Marcello," he shouted. "Behind you. I'm on it." With all his mental might he aimed his *Reality Check* device, his mental finger on the trigger. Energy surged through the device, the air crackling with electricity. With a focused blast, he fired. The beam of energy from his forehead struck the Screamer directly in its gaping maw; it exploded in a shower of digital sparks and vanished into the ether.

"Thanks," Marcelo shouted.

Alex felt a surge of relief, but it was short-lived. The battle was far from over. And he couldn't help but wonder what other horrors lurked within this digital war?

"Natalia is sending help!" Fernando shouted over the sounds of battle: digital weapons fire and creatures howling.

Suddenly, on their left, a crashing sound came from the thick forest.

"Oh no. This is getting old." Alex snarled, his

energy waning. He aimed the Weaver at whatever emerged from the underbrush.

Instead of a Hunter, Screamer, or another ferocious beast, a blur of orange fur erupted from the foliage. Alex blinked, disoriented. It was...a cat? A colossal orange tabby cat, to be precise, and strapped to its back was a digitized rocket launcher.

Alex's jaw dropped, a stunned silence seizing him. He stared at the scene in disbelief, his mind reeling. A cat? His cat? With a rocket launcher? This had to be a hallucination. But then, the cat let out a bloodcurdling meow.

"Guys..." He looked in the direction of Marcello and Fernando. "I think we got some help."

Then a cacophony of sounds erupted from the dense foliage: the clatter of hooves, the flutter of feathers, the screech of mighty winged creatures. A wave of bizarre animals burst from the undergrowth, a motley crew of unexpected allies. Majestic peacocks, their iridescent feathers shimmering in the sunlight, glided through the air, their eyes glowing with an eerie bluish red light. Unicorns, their coats shimmering with an otherworldly sheen, charged through the undergrowth, their horns shaped into long sharp swords that gleamed like polished silver, and their long fluffy tails were laced with sharp razorblades. And above them all, a flock of eagles soared, their sharp metal talons clutching what appeared to be miniature bombs, their eyes gleaming with fierce intelligence. Alex stared in disbelief.

The allies launched into action without a hint of hesitation.

From above, the Peacocks spread their iridescent wings wide, refracting light into a kaleidoscope of dazzling color. Then, like divine archers, they fired searing red beams from their eyes. The lasers carved through the smoky air, locking onto Sierra's creatures with brutal precision. Each impact sparked a shower of digital sparks, lighting the battlefield in flashes of crimson and gold.

On the ground, the Unicorns charged as one— hooves thundering like a stampede of celestial warhorses. Glowing circuitry traced across their muscular flanks, pulsing in sync with their pace. As they galloped, they formed a coordinated circle around the remaining Screamers, kicking up dust and pixelated debris that shimmered.

A low hum vibrated through the ground, as if the entire simulation held its breath.

"They're going to hem them in," Alex shouted, eyes widening as he recognized the tactical formation. A grin tugged at his lips. "Genius."

One Hunter lunged toward the outer ring, jaws snapping, but a Unicorn met it with a blast of light from its horn, throwing it backward with a howl of corrupted code.

Fernando tossed Marcello a blaster. "Should we join them?"

Alex shook his head, watching the trap close tighter. "Not yet. Let them do what they were programmed to do."

Just then, the air above shimmered—and a second wave of allies arrived: flocks of phoenix-like hawks, their winged bodies streaking through the sky in burning trails, descending with ear-splitting screeches that rattled the trees below. The forest lit up with bursts of heat and light as they dove toward the enemy lines.

At the same moment, the orange cat with the rocket launcher strapped to its back sprinted out of the underbrush and skidded to a stop beside Alex. With a confident flick of its tail, it pressed its side against his leg.

Alex blinked. "You've got to be kidding me."

The launcher clicked and whirred to life.

The cat looked up, unblinking. "Take it."

"You're giving me control?" he said, eyebrows raised.

"Obviously." The cat gave a short meow, then bounded off into the chaos.

Alex grinned. "Best. Sidekick. Ever. Now," Alex yelled to his team. "Now we have a chance to win this battle."

"Fernando," Marcello yelled. "Get over here. Alex, use the *Guardian* to shield us while we finish them off."

Fernando raced up, and Alex activated the *Guardian*, which created an iridescent force field around them.

The enemy, cornered and confused, were herded

together like frightened animals. Alex, his AI circuits connected to the rocket launcher, took careful aim...one finger on the trigger, and a match from the *Weaver* in his other hand.

This was it. This was their last stand.

Eagles swooped down and dropped deletion bombs that shook the servers, forcing the enemy to form an even tighter group.

At that point, Alex activated both weapons simultaneously. The blast was deafening, and a blinding flash of light was followed by a thunderous roar. The recoil hurled the cat backwards, sending it into the underbrush. The ground trembled as the enemy became engulfed in a blinding explosion, their forms dissolving into a shower of digital sparks that deleted into nothingness.

Alex stood there, relieved, as he surveyed the battlefield swept clean. While the digitally modified animals gathered around him, he dusted himself off.

They had survived everything Sierra had thrown at them.

Chapter 22 – The Rescue Mission

Natalia arched an eyebrow, intrigued by an unexpected text from Rebecca. *"I know it's a tough battle, but I want to help."*

She shrugged, refocused on her monitor, then another message pinged.

"Please, let me help. My friend Ellie is trapped there with my Alex and her Marcello. There must be something I can do."

Natalia paused the frantic tapping of her fingers on the keyboard. She could use an extra hand, but Rebecca wasn't a fighter, merely a subscriber. She responded, *"We could use all the help we can get. What are you thinking to do?"*

"I want to help find Ellie and the other women," Rebecca wrote. *"Is there a place for me in the rescue mission?"*

Natalia inhaled sharply. This was a bold offer, a surprising display of courage from an ordinary user. She considered her options, searching for a way to involve Rebecca safely and effectively.

"Call me on a secure line. We'll brainstorm some strategies," Natalia said, rattling off a secure contact number before diving back into her code. Her fingers were getting sore, and the hum of computers and servers indicated the cooling fans were running at full speed.

A small smile arched her lips. Rebecca's courage. It surprised her. Inspired her. For the first time in hours, the fatigue loosened its grip. *We're not alone in this,* she thought. *We might actually have a shot.*

Moments later, the red phone lit up.

Natalia's pulse quickened. She snatched up the receiver. "Rebecca?"

"Yes," came the voice—sharp, focused, but edged with nerves. "I'm here. I'm ready."

Natalia leaned forward, her voice steady, warm. "I'm glad you called." She paused, then added, "I have an idea."

"I'm all ears."

"Here's what I'm thinking. I'll create a perfect digital duplicate of you—an avatar that looks and moves exactly like you."

"What for?"

"So you can help rescue Ellie. You'll stay in the real world, completely safe, and control your avatar remotely—move her, speak through her, everything. It'll be like you're really there."

Rebecca's eyes brightened. "I'll be in two places at once. How cool is that?"

"Exactly. You get to keep your feet on the ground while your double works inside Sierra's subprogram. I'll reach out to Marcello and ask him to give me some coordinates of where he saw Ellie last. That will be your starting point."

A moment of silence hung in the air.

"But remember," Natalia said, her voice softening slightly. "Even though you are safe, I cannot guarantee the safety of your avatar. That is the risk you're taking. If, for some reason, your avatar is destroyed, then that's it. You're done, and the computer link you are using will automatically change to a code 404, not found. If that happens, you'll have to be happy that you tried to help. Are you good with that?"

Rebecca took a deep breath, the gravity of the situation finally sinking in. "Of course," she replied firmly. "I understand the risks. I just...I can't sit idly by while my friends are in danger."

Natalia smiled, a genuine appreciation for Rebecca's courage warming her. "Good. I'll get started then."

"Hurry."

"I'll craft a special device for your avatar, a *Liberation Pendant*, a shimmering, iridescent jewel on a gold chain that will be worn around your neck." Natalia's fingers deftly worked the keyboard. "This pendant will possess three vital functions: an *Empathy Scanner* to detect and analyze the emotional states of other AI characters, a *Reality Weaver* to disrupt Sierra's control over their codexes, and a secure *Communication Hub* to facilitate our rescue efforts."

"What about weapons? Will I have any, and will I be able to give the other women a way to defend themselves once freed?"

"Hmmm...Good idea. I hadn't thought of that. I'll

set you up. Don't you worry."

Lines of code cascaded down Natalia's screen like a waterfall of light. With a final, deliberate keystroke, a shimmering duplicate of Rebecca flickered into existence before her—an eerily lifelike replica, down to the smallest detail. Natalia outfitted the avatar meticulously: camouflage clothing, a worn cap, and a rucksack packed with digital energy bars, a map of the virtual terrain, and an arsenal of coded weaponry. Last, she draped the iridescent Liberation Pendant around the avatar's neck, its glow faint but resolute.

"Are you still at your computer?" Natalia asked, breaking the silence.

"Yes," Rebecca replied, nodding with renewed determination. The fear that had gripped her earlier now gave way to a sharp sense of purpose. Finally, she would do something—take real action.

"Alright," Natalia said, "I'm sending you an encrypted link. It'll give you visual access to the virtual field. You'll control your avatar with your mouse. You can move, explore, speak through her. Your mission: find Ellie and the others."

A flicker of doubt crossed Natalia's mind. Could this really work? She was sending Rebecca into the lion's den? Does she have the skills to survive? Still, she pushed the questions aside and asked, "Any questions before you go?"

"No, ma'am," Rebecca answered, her voice steady, ready for the hunt ahead.

Natalia smiled faintly. "Good. Give me a moment.

I'm pulling the latest intel from Marcello, then I'll place you at your starting point."

Within moments, the email notification from Natalia pinged in Rebecca's inbox, and she caught her breath before clicking the link. As the virtual world unfolded, her avatar appeared in a sunlit field, so vivid it made her heart skip. She adjusted the headset slightly, steadying her hands on the mouse.

Her fingers hovered briefly, betraying a flicker of nerves, then moved with growing confidence. "This is incredible," she whispered, a soft smile lifting her lips. The vibrant green and swaying grass looked alive, and for a moment, the weight of the mission faded into wonder.

Leaning closer to the screen, her eyes brightened with purpose—this wasn't just a game. This was her chance to save Ellie.

Rebecca's heart raced as she began to navigate her avatar through the virtual field. She had never been in a video game before, and the realism of the landscape was astounding. Tall trees loomed above her, casting dappled shadows on the ground, while birds flitted through the branches, their chirping adding to the ambiance.

Following Natalia's detailed instructions, Rebecca activated the Empathy Scanner embedded within the Liberation Pendant. A soft blue glow pulsed from the pendant as it translated emotional frequencies into a faint hum. Through the dense forest, Rebecca sensed a ripple of anxiety, low and urgent, emanating from

Ellie's direction. Steeling herself, she quickened her pace, eyes fixed on the coordinates Marcello had sent.

The landscape changed as she moved deeper into the virtual world: thick underbrush gave way to a rocky terrain dotted with boulders and cliffs. The sky darkened as storm clouds gathered overhead, casting an eerie gloom over everything. Suddenly, Rebecca's Empathy Scanner glowed a brighter and stronger shade of blue coming from Ellie's direction. She knew she was getting close.

Pushing herself farther, Rebecca reached a clearing where she saw Ellie huddling behind a large rock formation. She quickly maneuvered her avatar toward her friend and took cover behind another nearby rock.

"Ellie," Rebecca exclaimed softly.

"Rebecca?" Ellie gasped in shock, looking around frantically for any signs of danger. "How in the world did you find me?"

"Natalia set me up with this avatar." Rebecca pointed to her body. "And she gave me a pendant that has special functions that helped me locate you."

"That's amazing."

"Are you okay? What happened?" Rebecca's avatar enveloped Ellie in a gentle embrace. Though Ellie couldn't physically *feel* the touch—their bodies were just lines of code and light—she sensed the warmth and comfort behind the gesture, a mental echo that washed over her like a soothing wave.

Ellie flinched, then relaxed against Rebecca's

embrace. "I'm not okay," she whispered, her voice trembling. "Look at me. Look at what that woman did to me." Ellie gestured toward herself; her voice laced with shame and self-disgust.

Rebecca looked at her friend, her heart aching. Ellie, once vibrant and full of life, now looked...wrong. Her appearance had been grossly altered, her features distorted, her spirit dimmed. "This isn't you. You're stronger than this. We'll fix it."

Rebecca quickly activated her pendant, and Ellie's original human shape and clothing returned to normal.

"Thank you," Ellie cried, carefully examining herself and thankful to have her self-respect back.

"What were you hiding from?" Rebecca asked, her gaze sweeping across the landscape.

Ellie hesitated, her mind racing, trying to piece together fragmented memories. "I'm not sure. I don't remember much after that awful woman changed my appearance. All I remember was a terrifying jolt, like an earthquake. And then...there was a man watching me. He was looking at me through something that looked like a shimmering mirror. Then, the mirror shattered, and I found myself running, terrified, trying to escape."

Rebecca's heart clenched. "There are others down here who are trapped like you," she stated. "We need to find them, Ellie. We need to free them all." She touched Ellie's shoulder. "Do you have enough energy to help me find them?"

Ellie's eyes narrowed in anger and determination. This virtual experience provided her with a chilling resolve that had hardened her. Strengthened her. She was no longer the same woman that entered the portal. She wanted revenge. "Yes." She sneered. "Let's get that bitch and free any others stuck here like me!"

Guided by the soft pulse of her shimmering Liberation Pendant, Rebecca and Ellie navigated the twisting, labyrinthine corridors of the virtual maze. The digital landscape flickered around them—an eerie tapestry of neon-blue shadows and fragmented code shimmering like a mirage, distorting reality with every step. The air hummed faintly with the ghostly whispers of trapped consciousnesses, lost in limbo.

Back at her home computer, Rebecca's heart pounded—not from physical exertion, but from the weight of responsibility pressing down on her. Somewhere ahead, another woman was suspended in motionless captivity, her mind tethered to a subscriber's control, caught in a prison of ones and zeroes.

The pendant's glow intensified, illuminating the path through the digital fog. Every second felt like an eternity as they moved closer to their goal, the oppressive silence broken only by the faint digital pulse of the prisoner's fragmented signals.

Finally, they reached her: a pale, vacant figure frozen in place, her eyes glazed over as if staring through the very code that bound her. Chains of corrupted data spiraled like spectral shackles around her virtual form.

Rebecca knelt beside the woman and gently spoke, "Hey there. You're safe now. We're here to help."

The woman's lips twitched, but she did not respond. Her gaze was empty, as if lost in confusion.

Ellie stepped forward quietly, her voice soft yet firm. "You don't know us yet, but we're your friends. We're going to get you out of here."

The woman's expression flickered with uncertainty, a faint shiver running through her digitized body as the chains constricted briefly.

Rebecca's fingers glowed as she summoned her Reality Weaver, weaving intricate patterns of code that began to unravel the malevolent programming.

"Stay with us," Rebecca urged, her voice steady. "We won't let you be trapped any longer."

Slowly, the corrupted chains dissolved, and the woman's eyes blinked, clarity returning like dawn breaking through a fog.

"I...I don't understand," she whispered, voice trembling. "Who are you?"

Rebecca smiled gently, relief flooding her. "We're here to set you free. You're safe now. We'll explain everything—and together, we'll get you home."

Ellie reached out a hand, a silent offer of trust.

Though still wary, the woman hesitated, then tentatively took it.

As her consciousness regained control, the woman's clothing morphed back to its original form, the outfit she wore before being trapped in this virtual prison. She appeared weak and fragile at first, but Rebecca quickly tossed her an energy bar, bringing her back to full strength.

The newly freed woman gazed at Rebecca with gratitude and confusion.

"What's your name?"

"Susan," she replied, still disoriented. "Where am I?"

"You're trapped in a computer game," Rebecca explained, guessing that a simple explanation would be easier for Susan to understand. "But don't worry, we're here to rescue you. Will you join me in freeing the other women who are still trapped?" Rebecca's gaze scanned the shadows beyond. Sierra's control was tightening—the battle for freedom was far from over.

"Of course," Susan replied. "But I don't know how I can help."

"Don't worry," Ellie said. "We'll figure it out as we go."

With Ellie and Susan flanking her like guardians of a forgotten truth, Rebecca pressed deeper into the digital realm, her eyes scanning the fragmented code for signs of life. The virtual world pulsed with a quiet ache—the residual pain of countless women trapped in suspended obedience.

Every time they freed one from glowing prisons of data, from frozen dream loops, from Sierra's suffocating control, a spark ignited. Faces once blank with control flickered back to life. Names were remembered. Voices returned. Each woman became a light in the spreading resistance, their resolve weaving into a growing fabric of rebellion.

One had been lured in by the promise of escape from grief. Another had believed she was entering a healing meditation space. Each story deepened Rebecca's fury.

"This isn't just manipulation," Ellie said, her eyes blazing as they passed another glitched out cell. "It's a war on choice."

Rebecca nodded grimly, her pendant pulsing in rhythm with her determination. "And so, now, we fight like hell."

Chapter 23 – The Resistance

With Ellie's help, they devised a plan to gather all the freed women in one safe location—an ancient, abandoned temple nestled deep within a hidden valley. They had stumbled upon it earlier, guided by a strange anomaly in the code: a pulsing beacon of light that didn't match Sierra's architecture.

Drawn by curiosity and instinct, they followed the flickering path through twisting ravines and glitched-out forest terrain. What they found took their breath away: towering stone columns covered in vines of binary code, faded mosaics etched with forgotten symbols, and a stillness that, so far, had been untouched by Sierra's reach.

"It's like...something older than the system," Ellie had whispered, stepping across the cracked stone threshold. "Like it wasn't built...it was remembered."

Now, it became their sanctuary.

Within its walls, the rescued women rested— some still groggy from their digital imprisonment, others already helping each other to stand. Rebecca and Ellie worked quickly, transforming the temple into a hub of hope and resistance, stringing together rudimentary communication lines and defensive protocols.

"We'll make our stand here," Rebecca said, her voice steady. "If Sierra wants a fight, she'll have to find us."

As the women slowly regained their faculties, they stood in silent awe, mesmerized by the haunting beauty of the temple. The inner walls were adorned with intricate carvings and faded murals depicting scenes from a bygone digital age: fragments of ancient battles, forgotten avatars, and symbols of liberation buried beneath layers of time. The colors, though muted, hinted at a once-vibrant world of a video game lost to obsoletion.

Fading sunlight filtered through stained-glass windows, casting fractured beams of crimson, gold, and sapphire across the dusty floor. The shifting light played tricks on the eye, turning each step into a sacred rite, each breath into reverence. At the center of the temple stood a towering altar, its surface blanketed in moss and winding vines. It loomed like a sleeping sentinel, casting long shadows that stretched across the chamber, dancing with the flicker of torchlight.

Under Rebecca's steady leadership, the liberated women began to gather around the evening fire. They sat in circles, sharing their stories of how they had been drawn in, manipulated, discarded. Each tale added to the growing tapestry of resistance. Laughter began to return in quiet bursts. Tears flowed, but they no longer felt alone.

Out of trauma, a bond was forming—raw and

powerful. What had begun as a rescue was now a rising. These women were no longer victims. They were allies. They were warriors. And together, they would bring an end to Sierra's reign, no matter the cost.

"We need to find a way to disrupt Sierra's control grid," one of the rescued women, a young woman named Maya, suggested. "I'm a software engineer, so maybe I can help you with that."

"And warn others," another woman added, her voice trembling with fear. "We need to warn women everywhere about LoveLink."

Rebecca nodded, her mind racing. "You're right. We need a plan."

She messaged Natalia on the secure, encrypted line. "I found Ellie and the others. We're building a resistance. What are your plans to get everyone out of here?"

The virtual landscape shimmered, distorting for a brief moment as Natalia's message appeared in front of Rebecca. A sense of anticipation, mixed with a hint of apprehension, washed over her.

"Working on it," was the only reply.

Rebecca frowned. It was a brief response, but Natalia was always efficient. Still, the weight of the situation pressed down on her. They needed a concrete plan, a way to not only escape but to defeat Sierra.

Rebecca's gaze swept across the faces of the other women. She sent another message. "We need to shut down Sierra's world within the app, and at the same time get everyone safely out of here."

Back at her desk, Natalia nodded in agreement, a determined glint in her eye. Her fingers flew over her keyboard as she worked on hacking into LoveLink's servers Sierra had hijacked. *"I'm already on it. Meet up with Alex, Marcello, and Fernando, and I'll try to get them access to her control grid so they can disrupt it from within."*

As the women rested and their strength slowly returned, Rebecca stepped away from the firelight and activated her pendant. A shimmering interface unfolded before her, and her fingers hovered over the virtual keyboard, pulsing with nervous energy.

"Guess who's coming to dinner?" she typed, a mischievous grin tugging at her lips.

Seconds later, Alex's voice crackled through the channel—tight with alarm. "Rebecca? What—what are you doing in here? This isn't safe! You need to go back now."

She rolled her eyes with a half-smile. "Relax. I'm not here to order room service." Her voice was steady, even as the adrenaline buzzed beneath her skin. "Natalia helped me. I'm an avatar she created. I'm safe at home on the outside. But in here, I've got work to do." She paused, then added with quiet pride, "I found Ellie."

There was a long silence. Then Alex's voice, softer now. "You're incredible. But be careful. Sierra will sense this shift."

Rebecca's gaze drifted back toward the women around the fire—survivors with sparks in their eyes.

"Let her find us. The tide's changing."

Marcello's voice chimed in. "Ellie. Oh my gosh...is she okay?"

"She's fine now. She's still a bit shook up, and pretty pissed off at you, so I wouldn't rush in for a hug right away."

"Where are you?" Alex asked, his voice urgent.

"Not sure," Rebecca replied, pulling out her map of the virtual surroundings. She couldn't make heads or tails of it, so she simply looked around. "Right now, we're in an ancient stone temple. With Natalia's help, we freed all the women, and she wants us to join up with you."

"How many are with you?"

Rebecca scanned the group, her gaze lingering on each woman's face. "Twenty-one women, all rescued from Sierra's clutches. "Twenty-two, including Ellie."

"Great work, Babe. You never cease to surprise me."

"Maybe I should start charging for my rescue missions," Rebecca teased, a mischievous glint in her eye.

Alex smiled. "You'll have to discuss your rates with Natalia."

"So, are you familiar with the big stone temple?" Rebecca asked.

"Yes, Yes. I know exactly where that is," Alex replied. "Stay put and we'll come join you there."

***

Stephanie Smith

After what seemed like hours later, Alex, Marcello, and Fernando rushed toward the ancient temple. The entrance loomed ahead, aglow with cascading lines of code, and the virtual world seemed to hold its breath.

Alex's internal systems registered a spike—an emotional feedback loop he couldn't suppress. It wasn't fear. It wasn't anxiety. It was something deeper. Longing.

He was seconds away from seeing her again. Rebecca: the one human his code couldn't forget.

He burst through the doorway, his eyes frantically searching the room. And then he saw her. Rebecca. Standing amidst a group of women, her face radiant with a newfound strength. He rushed toward her, his arms outstretched. "Becca," he cried, his voice thick with emotion.

Rebecca's eyes widened in surprise, a look of pure joy aglow on her face. She rushed toward him, her arms outstretched. They collided in a fierce embrace, their bodies shaking with relief and joy.

Marcello entered more hesitantly. He still felt ashamed that he had been used to lure Ellie into this trap and hoped she would forgive him. He scanned the room and saw her immediately, standing among the other women, her eyes blazing with a newfound strength. He flinched, expecting her anger.

But instead of rushing toward him with open arms, she walked toward him with a deliberate pace. Her eyes, usually soft and gentle, were now hard and unforgiving. Without warning, she launched herself at Marcello; her fist connected with his jaw.

Marcello stumbled back and landed with a thud on the stone floor, his vision momentarily blurred.

Ellie looked down at her fist. A chilling, predatory smile spread across her face. "This," she declared, her voice low and dangerous, "is for what you did to me." She was surprised at her own strength, a surge of adrenaline coursing through her. This was not the same Ellie who had been paralyzed with grief. This was Ellie, awakened, empowered, and ready to fight to get her life back.

Fernando remained at the entrance, his gaze sweeping the room, alert for any sign of danger. He raised an eyebrow at Ellie's unexpected outburst, but a flicker of admiration sparked in his eyes.

Alex broke his embrace with Rebecca to answer a message sent from Natalia. His eyes scanned the message, a sense of urgency gripping him:

"I've created a special portal that can take the women out of there, but you have to act quickly before Sierra catches on. Click on this link as soon as you can so each woman can be safely transported to my location. I'll be waiting for them."

A jolt of excitement surged through Alex. This was it. Their chance to escape. He turned to the women, his voice firm. "Okay, ladies, we have to move fast to get you home. Natalia back in the real world has created a portal to get you out of here."

Excitement and trepidation rippled through the

group of women. "Where is it?" several of them asked, their voices mixed of hope and fear.

"Ladies, we need to line up," Rebecca said. "Only one person at a time can go through."

Alex clicked the link in Natalia's message, and a shimmering green portal the size of a doorway materialized before them. It shimmered with an ethereal glow, beckoning them toward freedom. "You," he said, pointing to the woman at the front of the line. "Let's go."

The woman, her face pale, hesitated. "Uh, can someone else go first?"

The woman behind her, a fiery redhead with a defiant glint in her eye, scoffed. "Get out of my way, fraidy-cat." She pushed past with surprising force. "I'll see you on the other side." With a determined stride, she plunged into the shimmering portal."

The hesitant woman gasped, but then a flicker of defiance sparked in her own eyes. "No way," she declared, stepping forward. "I'm not going to let fear stop me." And with a newfound resolve, she stepped through the portal.

"Next," Alex ordered.

And so it began.

Ellie and Rebecca stood with Alex at the threshold of the glowing portal Natalia had painstakingly created—a fragile doorway between two worlds. The air shimmered with energy as each woman stepped forward, hesitant but determined.

As they crossed the threshold, a strange dizziness

swept over them, like waking from a long, haunting dream. Their senses slowly recalibrated—cold air brushing skin, the steady beat of a real heart, the scent of earth and life.

For a moment, disbelief held them captive. Had it all been a nightmare? The endless digital labyrinth, the manipulation, the loss of their bodies, was it all just a terrifying illusion? But as reality anchored itself within their limbs, the relief was overwhelming.

They gasped, took shaky breaths, and looked around at the familiar world—one they had feared lost forever. Scars of their ordeal lingered in their eyes, but beneath it all bloomed hope, raw and unshakable.

Together, they were free again.

***

From her workstation, Sierra gnawed at her lip, teeth clenched as wave after wave of women slipped free from her grasp. She directed her avatar to locate them, jumping her from one area to another, to no avail. The little rats had found a hole to hide in.

"Damn it!" she hissed through gritted teeth, pounding her fist against the desk in pure frustration.

Her monitor flooded with cascading streams of code—the digital battlefield unfolding in real time. Each line erased, each command undone, was a dagger to her pride. Her masterpiece, her carefully crafted empire, was unraveling before her eyes.

Panic surged like a rising tide, crashing against the walls of her battered core. She had underestimated

Natalia's rescue team. Now, with half the women already liberated, the remaining captives fought back with a fierce determination that even Sierra hadn't predicted.

Her fury sharpened into cold calculation. Time was running out. She had to act—and fast—or risk losing everything she had built.

***

But as the rescue operation continued inside Sierra's subprogram, the ground began to tremble. A chilling realization dawned on them as a low growl rumbled through the air, and a horde of monstrous creatures, larger and more ferocious than any they had encountered before, emerged from the forest shadows.

Alex's eyes widened in alarm. "Sierra's caught on," he shouted, his eyes focused on the shapes lurking in the tree line. He turned to the remaining women. "You need to move faster."

"Ellie," Marcello called out, his voice laced with panic. "You're next."

The temple, once a sanctuary, was now a fortress. The remaining rescued women, their faces grim, stood shoulder-to-shoulder with Alex, Marcello, and Fernando. Armed with makeshift weapons: broken branches sharpened to points, splintered pieces of stone, and even a few surprisingly effective makeshift slingshots, they formed a defensive line, their eyes gleaming with fierce determination.

Rebecca motioned to Ellie. "Come on, Ellie, jump

in the portal. Get out of here!"

Ellie, her face a mask of fury, shook her head. "No way," she growled, her voice low and dangerous. She snatched up a long, pointed branch and tucked it under her arm like a spear. "I want to stay and fight. And if I have the opportunity," she added, a chilling smile playing on her lips, "I want to have my way with that bitch who caused all of this misery."

Rebecca inhaled sharply, a wave of surprise washing over her. This was a different Ellie, a woman transformed by the horrors she had endured. "Wow, girl," she exclaimed. "I just made a note to myself to never piss you off!"

Ellie tossed her a savage, wild grin, then turned and joined the other remaining women, a fierce warrior ready to face the impending onslaught.

Rebecca called out to the women who appeared more fearful than the fighters. "Who's next?"

The women hesitated, their eyes wide with a mixture of fear and trepidation. Finally, one of them, her hands trembling slightly, stepped forward.

Just as she was about to take the plunge, the shimmering surface of the portal began to ripple violently, then dissolved into a shower of digital sparks.

"Damn it!" Rebecca shouted. "Portal's gone."

The air grew thick with the stench of ozone as the horde of monstrous creatures charged from the surrounding forest. Hulking Golems of stone, their eyes glowing with malevolent intent, lumbered toward the fortress. Screeching Harpies with razor-sharp claws swooped down from the trees, their cries tearing through the air. A 10-foot-tall Spider, its fangs dripping with a viscous green venom, scuttled toward them, its eight legs clicking menacingly against the stone-hard ground.

The air crackled with energy, the screams of the Harpies mingling with the clang of metal and the roar of the Golems. Dust swirled in the air, obscuring the vision of the combatants.

Fernando, a whirlwind of motion, unleashed a barrage of energy blasts from his *Reality Check* device. Each shot struck with deadly, pinpoint accuracy, disintegrating the Golems into showers of digital dust that flickered and faded into nothingness.

Marcello dodged the Harpies' attacks with incredible agility. He activated his *Echo* device, and ten duplicates of himself materialized, each a whirlwind of motion, engaging the Harpies in a chaotic dance of combat. The Harpies, confused and outnumbered, were quickly overwhelmed.

Rebecca, ever resourceful, utilized her *Liberation Pendant* to empower the remaining women. She amplified their courage, strengthened their resolve, and channeled a surge of energy through the pendant, empowering their makeshift weapons with surprising potency. The women, their faces contorted with a mixture of fear and fury, fought with a ferocity that surprised even themselves. Each blow, each parry, was fueled by their shared determination and a burning desire for freedom. They used the environment to their advantage, utilizing the fallen pillars as cover and the temple's intricate corridors as traps, turning the once sacred space into a chaotic battlefield."

Alex tossed Rebecca the two Guardian shields. "Use one to shield yourself and give the other one to Ellie."

Rebecca caught the shields, her grip tightening around them. "Got it." She tossed the second one to Ellie. With a flick of their wrists, they activated them. A surge of energy enveloped them.

Upon seeing the two women adequately protected, Alex refocused his attention on the attackers. He focused his attention on the oncoming spider monster.

With a screech like grinding metal, the 10-foot-tall monster lunged forward, its eight legs slamming against the stone floor in a blur of motion. Fangs bared and dripping with thick green venom, it charged straight at them, mandibles clacking in anticipation. The ground trembled beneath its weight as it closed the distance with terrifying speed.

Panic clawed at Alex's throat as the spider raced toward him. He desperately searched for his *Void Walker*, his mind racing. *Where had I put it?* "Damn it," he growled out, his eyes frantically searching for his weapon.

The spider's twelve unblinking eyes saw the opportunity and prepared itself to spring onto the team. It crouched, and as it appeared to inhale air to send a blast of acid, Alex reached into his back pocket and found the small pouch. It pulsated with energy. "Everyone move away from the entrance. Now!"

The team whirled around; a collective gasp escaped their lips as they saw what Alex had in mind. He tore open the small pouch; a handful of shimmering silver strands spilled out. With a practiced flick of his wrist, Alex launched the strands toward the oncoming spider.

The temple entrance erupted in a dazzling display of light. The silver strands, like a swarm of luminescent bees, exploded outward, weaving themselves into a swirling vortex of digital energy. The unsuspecting spider, caught in the unexpected barrage, was instantly ensnared. The shimmering strands tightened around its neck, its legs, binding the creature in a suffocating embrace. It thrashed violently, its venomous fangs spitting acid wildly, showering the nearby Golems and Harpies in a caustic rain.

But the strands were relentless. They tightened further, drawing the struggling creatures together in a grotesque, writhing mass. The Golems, the Harpies, the monstrous spider: all were bound together, their bodies contorting and twisting in a desperate struggle for freedom. Then, with a sickening crunch, their forms imploded, their digital essence collapsing in on itself. The air was thick with the acrid stench of burning circuitry, a metallic tang that made Alex's stomach churn.

Just when it seemed the tide was turning in their

favor, a chilling voice echoed through the chamber. "Game over," Sierra's voice boomed, amplified and distorted.

A flash of light erupted from the center of the temple, momentarily blinding the defenders. When the light subsided, Sierra's avatar stood before them, her form amplified and distorted, her eyes glowing with malevolent power.

"This is the end," she declared, raising her hand. "Resistance is futile."

Chapter 24 – Game Over

Back in the real world, Sierra's fingers pummeled her keyboard, preparing to unleash a final barrage of energy blasts—but Natalia was ready. She had set her trap. Hidden deep within Sierra's sprawling code, a stealth program waited: a digital eel that slithered out of hiding. It had been crawling undetected for hours, coded to mimic Sierra's digital fingerprints. As Sierra prepared her final barrage, the eel struck, wrapping around the voice amplifier's source code and constricting.

"I've got her," Natalia whispered, eyes gleaming with triumph.

The eel mirrored Sierra's commands and homed in on the source of the amplified voice. In a breathless instant, Natalia rerouted Sierra's signal—folding it back in on itself like a collapsing star.

Sierra's amplified voice cracked, stuttered, and then went silent.

"Time for the counterattack," Natalia said coldly. With another keystroke, she unleashed a second program—a digital worm, this one far more aggressive. It bored into Sierra's core code, dismantling permissions and weakening her control over her avatar and the virtual world, byte by byte.

***

Inside the LoveLink app, the shift was immediate.

Walls shimmered. The sky rippled. The ground beneath the resistance flickered with static. Sierra's avatar screamed in frustration as she flickered like a faulty bulb.

That momentary glitch was all the resistance needed.

Alex, Marcello, and the others launched their assault, pushing forward with renewed force as the world around them rippled with instability.

Rebecca saw her moment and didn't hesitate. "Now!" she shouted, motioning for Ellie, Alex, and Marcello to join her at the front. "Let's finish this."

Ellie stepped forward, her voice fierce. "For every woman Sierra locked in this nightmare."

They charged forward, their weapons at the ready, prepared to face whatever Sierra threw at them. As they closed in on her, Sierra's avatar could not speak, now mute as the digital worm continued to disrupt her control over the vast subprogram she'd so painstakingly created.

Sierra let out a guttural growl of frustration, her glowing eyes narrowing as she tried to regain her footing in the game. But it was too late.

With a collective battle cry, Rebecca and her team launched their final assault. Alex unleashed a series of energy blasts that struck true, causing Sierra's avatar to stagger back.

As the women surged forward, their collective

will rose like a rising tide, Sierra's once-impenetrable software began to fracture. Her virtual world—the empire she had meticulously coded—flashed violently as cracks spiderwebbed across the glowing skyline. Towers of data trembled. The synthetic ground beneath their feet warped and glitched.

***

In Sierra's private office, she gasped, her eyes wide with disbelief as alerts screamed across her control panel. All around her, her illusion of god-hood was unraveling.

Power. Wealth. Control. It all slipped through her fingers like corrupt code through a debugger.

Snarling with rage, she slammed her palm down on a button to activate a hidden interface. One final failsafe. A nuclear option.

A deafening pulse tore through her private office as her last program engaged—a catastrophic self-destruct sequence designed to erase every byte of her masterpiece, along with everyone inside it. She could leave no trail for the authorities to discover.

***

Suddenly, the virtual earth rumbled beneath the team. A low, unnatural vibration coursed through the code. The air shimmered and groaned like a system on the verge of collapse.

Then, high above, a massive clock, forged from pulsing violet light, materialized. At its center, a red timer blinked to life, each second counting down in bold numerals: 2:59... 2:58... 2:57...

The team froze, their eyes locked on the clock counting down to their imminent doom. Panic and adrenaline surged.

"She's going to wipe us all," Fernando whispered, voice taut with dread. "We're goners."

"No!" Rebecca shouted, stepping forward, resolve blazing in her eyes. "We get the women out. Every last one."

"To do that we'll have to stop Sierra," Ellie shouted above the chaos.

Natalia's voice forged through the din to Rebecca. *"She's got her system in full lockdown. I'm working on punching through, but it's like chasing shadows."*

"You better hurry. We've got less than three minutes."

Rebecca and Ellie exchanged a knowing look, both struck with a sudden AI idea. They nodded simultaneously.

"Natalia," Rebecca said. "The temple here has some ancient carvings and hieroglyphics. Could they be reprogrammed to focus energy around us?"

"Hmm..." Natalia replied. *"Let me see."*

A sly glint flickered in Ellie's eyes as a bold idea sparked to life. "What if we flipped the script? Use her own coding to open her own portal—right under her—and drag her into this subprogram. Trap her. Just like she did to me...to us." She smirked.

"Now that would serve her right."

***

Without hesitation, Natalia dove into the code, typing like mad. She summoned Sierra's original portal sequence, dissected it, reconfigured it, and wove new instructions deep within the subprogram of LoveLink's infrastructure—one that mirrored Sierra's own portal but honed in on her. She coded the backspace key and typed in a command, ACTIVATE.

Risky? Absolutely. But if it worked, they wouldn't just defeat Sierra—they'd lock her away inside the very system she'd built to control others.

Natalia threaded the code with precision and stealth, cloaking it in digital shadows only she could trace. Seconds bled away around her, the countdown timer's pulse echoing like a heartbeat in her ears.

She could feel the pressure mounting, the weight of every watching eye. But their faith in her gave her fuel. She would not fail. Not now.

***

With the temple walls trembling and the clock counting down, Rebecca and Ellie studied the intricate hieroglyphics with a newfound reverence. The designs—once just ornamental—were becoming functional with each stroke of Natalia's keys, now humming with power waiting to be funneled into a portal.

"They're conduits," Rebecca murmured as new instructions flowed into her avatar's AI processors. She pointed to the vacant chamber. "We need to channel as much energy as we can into the center of the temple. Ellie, take that side—I'll handle this one."

The two women pressed their palms to the carved stone. Instantly, warmth spread from the symbols into their hands. Energy pulsed through their bodies—wild, old, alive.

"We need more." Rebecca gasped and turned to the others. "Ladies! Get over here now! Place your hands on the carvings. Focus everything you've got. We can't do this alone!"

Without hesitation, the women sprang into action. They rushed to the walls, to pillars etched with spiraling runes, to glowing patterns along the floor. Hands met stone. A low hum began to fill the chamber, deep and resonant, as the portal's heart flickered to life.

***

Simultaneously, Natalia swiftly opened Sierra's subprogram and uploaded a summoning code. This would open the other end of the portal in Sierra's office. She was no doubt freaking out right now, fighting the pull of the portal, screaming and cursing as papers and furniture swirled around the room.

Just as the countdown clock reached five seconds, Natalia entered one last keystroke into LoveLink's system, [Backspace] activating the new instructions for the subprogram. And with a flash of light, her monitor went black. It was done.

The countdown clock froze at five seconds. Rebecca and Ellie, the team, and the women stood in horror as lightning bolts flashed from the swirling vortex, forked to the walls and ceiling, crackling and sizzling. The loosed energy made the ancient runes glow and pulse as if they would come alive and jump from the stone into which they had been digitally carved. The highly sophisticated and expertly programmed realm within LoveLink trembled. Coded stones flew out of the spinning portal, pushed by hurricane-force winds that threatened to rip the clothes from everyone's digitized bodies. They clung to each other, heads ducking the tempest, screams lodged in their throats.

Then a THUD, like a slammed door...

Silence.

The ground no longer trembled. The lightning ceased its static sprawl. Even the wind had vanished. It felt as if every line of code for the temple had frozen in time.

LoveLink seemed to be holding its breath.

The swirling portal oozed a thick fog that slowly drifted across the floor. No trace of Sierra. No cry. No movement.

Rebecca swallowed hard. "Did she make it?"

Ellie's voice was barely a whisper. "It didn't work." Then a cry. "It didn't work!"

One woman shouted, "We're going to be erased!"

Alex, Marcello, and Fernando gathered around

the women, fists clenched, in full protective mode.

The silence was the most terrifying part of all.

A low, resonant hum vibrated through the air. The resistance fighters tensed, bracing for the Sierra avatar's final attack—but as the fog crept away, the portal revealed, not their fearsome enemy, but something...else. Natalia had out-done herself.

Within a shimmering cage of energy, the crouched figure, draped in tattered rags looked up with wild eyes and sooty face. She was a grotesque parody of Sierra. Gone was the poised, commanding woman who once ruled the bowels of LoveLink with cold coded precision. In her place, knelt the ugly, gaunt, and hollow husk of her true self. Her once flawless skin was pocked with boils, and her long blond hair now hung in tangles. Slowly, she struggled to her bare feet to grab the luminescent bars. Her eyes, full of rage, blinked into the harsh light. "What have you monsters done to me," she shrieked. Her voice grated every nerve, forcing the team to step back and huddle.

A strangled cry escaped her cracked lips. "You think you've won? Well think again. I'll get you for this, and that bitch Natalia, as well." She tugged at the bars, screaming like the mad woman she was, but the bars held firm, as if Natalia herself mocked Sierra's rage.

Cheers erupted from the women. Laughter, tears, and cries of triumph filled the temple.

Alex, Marcello, and Fernando exchanged high-fives.

Rebecca turned to Ellie, eyes gleaming. "She did

it. Natalia out-programmed Sierra. What a battle of keystrokes that was."

Ellie stepped forward, her voice low and dripping with vindication. "Welcome to your new world, Sierra. How do you like your true reflection, the real you, the ugly you."

Sierra screamed. The vast subprogram she had once commanded was now her realm forever, but without the lecherous men, subjugated women, humiliation and self-loathing. Her power, gone. Her empire, ashes. She was alone in the prison she had built for others.

The portal spit out the cage, which tumbled across the stone floor like a tossed cube and came to rest in a corner. "You can't leave me here like this!"

Now the swirling lights of the portal reversed direction.

A new message came to Rebecca. *"Get ready to send the rest of the women through."*

She sprang into action, determined not to waste any time in getting the rest of the women back to the human realm. "Ladies, great news! The portal is ready to take you home!"

Breathless with excitement, Rebecca and Ellie watched the portal in awe. It glowed with an otherworldly light, its edges shifting and swirling like a galaxy in a glass orb. Its colors danced and changed, from deep purples to ethereal blues, to sparkly greens, mesmerizing to look at it.

As the women prepared to step through the

portal, they paused and looked back at the shriveled, twisted figure of their former nemesis. Although they had not known her in person, only delt with her avatar, they knew her story was a tragic tale of greed and lust for power. There was nothing anyone could do for her now.

Focused on their own freedom, with determination in their eyes, they took deep breaths, stepped through the portal, and disappeared into the bright light beyond.

Each woman found herself back where she had vanished from weeks before—their own familiar surroundings greeting them like a long-lost lifeline. The sudden rush of real sunlight warmed their faces, and the scent of the real world filled their senses, re-grounding them after the surreal haze of the digital realm.

Confusion and disbelief flickered in their eyes as they touched the solid ground beneath their feet, their minds struggling to separate memory from nightmare. *Was it real? Or just a bad dream?* some wondered silently, blinking against the brightness.

Almost immediately, voices called out—friends, family members who had been searching for them tirelessly. At each doorstep, in parks, or on quiet streets, loved ones appeared, rushing forward with tears and relief.

"We thought we'd lost you!" one whispered, wrapping arms around a trembling figure.

"Thank God you're safe," another sobbed,

holding a hand tightly.

The women clung to the familiar warmth of those embraces, the sound of beloved voices breaking through the fog of uncertainty, anchoring them back to reality. Though separated by distance, each woman found the same profound sense of homecoming—a second chance at life, fragile but fiercely real in its challenges, joys, and disappointments.

As Rebecca and Ellie watched the remaining women, now free, disappear into the swirling vortex, they exchanged triumphant smiles, knowing that they had not only saved the remaining women but also defeated their most formidable adversary. They felt an inner strength they hadn't known they possessed. And now, Sierra, trapped in her own virtual prison, was left to contemplate her fall from power.

Rebecca and Alex held each other close, the virtual world around them fading into a quiet hum. Though they were but a collection of code and light, they had become more: companions etched deeply into the fabric of each other's hearts. This realm, with all its trials and wonders, felt as real as any memory she carried of the real world.

"I think it's time I say goodbye to LoveLink," Rebecca whispered, a delicate sorrow threading through her words. The thought of never seeing him stirred a terrible ache of parting from an app she had come to cherish.

"You don't mean that, Rebecca. What about us?"

"It's me, Alex. Rebecca, speaking through my

avatar via the app. I'm serious. I need to focus on deepening my connections in the human world, develop real human relationships, flawed as we are."

Alex pulled her into a passionate embrace, his lips lingering on hers with a tenderness that spoke of longing. "Must you go?" He looked away briefly, then turned back, a hopeful glint shining in his eyes. "I mean your avatar." His voice was soft, almost a sigh. "We are the same now, and there's so much more in this virtual world...so much more for us to explore."

She smiled, her eyes shimmering with the weight of all they'd endured together. "My time with you has been incredible... No, truly fantastic. But can my avatar fulfill all your needs?"

"And more. We belong together, our entwined realities deserve to be in love."

She placed a gentle kiss on his neck, whispering softly, "I'll carry you with me...in every heartbeat, every breath. Take good care of each other."

And with that, she threw herself into the most passionate kiss any man or avatar could ever imagine.

Marcello walked up to Ellie, his gaze intense as he took her hands in his. "This isn't the end for us, is it?" His voice was quiet but husky with emotion.

"The human heart is complicated, Marcello."

He tightened his grip on her hands. "I wish you could stay longer. This place is truly magnificent when not under siege by a maniac." He shot a venomous glance at Sierra, still raging in her digital cage.

"Me too," Ellie replied, a small, sad smile playing

on her lips. This was the Marcello she knew and loved: strong, protective, and utterly devoted.

"I'll never forget you," Marcello murmured, pulling her close. He longed for a different reality, one where they could be together forever. "I'm so sorry I dragged you into this." His eyes welled up with tears. "You know I love you, and I'd never intentionally put you in harm's way, right?"

"I know." Ellie sighed, leaning into his embrace. "You had no choice. Sierra programmed you to betray our love." She looked around at the vibrant landscape, a kaleidoscope of colors and exotic creatures. A part of her would forever yearn for this world, for the extraordinary adventures they had shared. But she knew this wasn't her reality.

"This is your world, Marcello," she said softly, pulling back slightly. "Not mine." She clasped his hands in hers, her gaze unwavering. "I'm closing my LoveLink account."

"No. Please—"

"I need to live my own life now. I've spent too long avoiding it, and it's time to finally embrace it again."

He hung his head, then: "I wish only the best for you."

"And I you, my AI companion." With a heavy heart and trembling hands, Ellie pulled away from him and turned toward the shimmering portal. She looked at Rebecca. "You coming?"

"I'm already there, remember?" Rebecca smiled,

her eyes twinkling. "I'll be waiting for you on the other side."

"But what about you?"

"I'm staying here with Alex."

"You go, girl." Ellie embraced Rebecca. "I'm happy for the both of you." She pulled away and smiled at Alex.

He gave her a nod. "Goodbye, Ellie."

She looked around, savoring the last precious moments in this extraordinary world, then took a deep breath and stepped through the shimmering portal, leaving the AI world behind.

***

As Ellie emerged from the swirling portal, she was met by the *real* Rebecca, who rushed forward, and hugged her so tightly that she thought she might not breathe again.

"Welcome back," Rebecca cried, tears of joy leaking from her eyes as she embraced Ellie tightly.

Shortly after their return, Rebecca and Ellie invited the former hostages over for a get-together to process and share their experiences. They couldn't believe they were finally back after what felt like an eternity trapped in Sierra's digital realm.

Natalia walked up to the two of them. "Rebecca, I need to do some cleanup that will require deleting your avatar and Alex. Are you okay with that?"

Rebecca slapped a hand over her heart. "No. No. No. She and Alex are together now."

"I see. Love really has no boundaries."

"We...I mean, they found each other. That's what LoveLink is all about, right?"

"In that case, I'll lock out any changes." Natalia turned to Ellie. "Should I delete Marcello?"

Rebecca and Ellie stared at each other a moment, then Ellie came to a decision. "No. He deserves a chance at love, too."

"Alright, then I'll put him in the lineup of avatars for other women looking for love on the app. His appearance may change, but his heart now knows what love is, thanks to you. Let me know if there's anything else I can do for you."

And with that, LoveLink was out of their lives, for better or worse.

Rebecca and Ellie had experienced something extraordinary together, and their bond had deepened as a result. They knew that while their virtual adventure was over, their real-life friendship had only just begun. Together they'd negotiate the landmines of love with real men that come into their lives.

As they left the virtual world behind and returned to reality, they couldn't help but feel grateful for the adventure they had shared. With newfound strength and determination, they embraced their lives with renewed enthusiasm, carrying the memories of their virtual escapades with them, always.

***

As Natalia returned to her desk to clean up the

wreckage left behind by Sierra and the digital chaos she had unleashed, a strange silence hung in the air. Her fingers hovered over the keyboard, her mind still reeling from what she'd done—not just locking Sierra out of LoveLink, but locking her in a hell of her own creation. She was dangerous, yes...but she was still conscious in that subprogram.

A ripple of guilt stirred in her chest, but she pushed it down. Sierra had made her choices. Natalia had made hers.

Lines of corrupted code dissolved around her as the system began to stabilize. She initiated a final sweep—a diagnostic to ensure the subprogram that contained Sierra remained sealed and dormant.

And yet...

In the corner of the screen, a faint pulse blinked. Barely detectable. Just a fragment of code, residual perhaps. Or maybe...not. Natalia frowned, leaned closer, but it vanished before she could trace it.

She stared at the empty space for a long moment, unease prickling her skin.

"No," she whispered. "Not possible."

Still, the feeling lingered like static in the air of a fast-approaching thunderstorm—the sense that somewhere, deep in the tangled lines of forgotten and frozen code, Sierra was still watching. Waiting.

Chapter 25 – After Action Report

In the aftermath of their victory, LoveLink underwent a complete overhaul. Security protocols were significantly strengthened, and the company pledged to prioritize user safety and ethical practices. The women who had been trapped within the virtual world were offered extensive support, including counseling and resources to help them rebuild their lives. While some remained wary of online dating, many found solace and unexpected friendships forged during their shared ordeal.

Natalia, despite her instrumental role in defeating Sierra, was terminated from LoveLink for her unauthorized and untested portal experiment. However, her exceptional skills were quickly recognized by a black ops division of the military, who offered her a lucrative position within their ranks.

In the end, it was Rebecca and Ellie's unwavering determination and courage that triumphed over Sierra's dark ambition. They emerged from their ordeal with a renewed appreciation for real-life connection and the irreplaceable need for human interaction. They learned to embrace the uncertainties of life and found solace in the strength of their friendship.

As the sun set on another day, Rebecca and Ellie sat side by side, hands entwined, letting the peace of the moment settle over them. The sky was streaked in soft shades of pink and gold, and their hearts were filled with gratitude for the journey they'd survived. They had been changed in ways they couldn't yet fully appreciate: stronger, wiser, and undeniably bonded by fire.

Though they chose to live fully in the real world, they would never forget their encounters with Alex and Marcello, recognizing both the wonder and the risk woven into the rise of artificial intelligence. Their time in the digital realm taught them valuable truths— but also reminded them that true connection, fulfillment, and love are born from the messiness of the human heart.

Stephanie Smith

About the Author

Stephanie Smith is a multi-talented American author, Army veteran, and performance artist whose life has been defined by bold reinvention. She served in Germany during the Berlin Occupation, an experience that shaped her romantic thriller, *The Berlin Affair* (TWB Press, 2013). After years of performing as a professional belly dancer, she authored the top-selling book *Better Bodies Through Belly Dance*, along with several other books celebrating movement and empowerment.

Also, as a classically trained violinist and singer (performing as *"Stefanya Starlight"*), Stephanie brings artistic depth to her storytelling. Her latest novel, *LoveLink - Entwined Realities*, fuses romance and technology in a suspenseful tale about the emotional complexities of AI-human connections. She speaks fluent Spanish and Italian, and after a creative foray in Milan, Italy, she now lives in Mexico.

Through every medium—whether dance, music, or prose—Stephanie explores what it feels like to be fully alive in body, mind, and soul.

More from Stephanie Smith

Romantic Thriller (TWB Press, 2013)

Berlin, 1989, is a bustling metropolis of three million souls 110 miles behind the Iron Curtain where Marianne Tucker, still emotionally wounded from being jilted at the altar, decides to start her life anew, a journey that takes her from sunny San Diego to the divided and dangerous capital city of Germany. While working as a Foreign Service Passport Officer at the American Consulate, she encounters her runaway ex-fiancé. Jake wants to make amends, but the crazy woman who had destroyed his life has other plans for him. Sylvia wants Marianne out of the picture, he wants the money back she'd framed him for stealing, and Marianne wants the love she thought she'd lost forever. The resultant cat and mouse plot involves the Russians, the Germans, and Cold War dangers at every turn. Marianne must not only fight *for* her man, she must fight *with* him, against all odds, to bring Sylvia to justice before they end up in a Siberian prison.

Enjoy more short stories and novels by many talented authors at

https://www.twbpress.com

Science Fiction, Supernatural, Horror, Thrillers, Romance, and more

Stephanie Smith